]

A
e:
i
h
h
a
n
B

k
t
h

MARY STOLZ

Bartholomew Fair

decorations by

PAMELA JOHNSON

BEECH TREE BOOKS

NEW YORK

Library of Congress Cataloging-in-Publication Data
Stolz, Mary (date)
Bartholomew Fair / by Mary Stolz.
   p.   cm.
Summary: On an August day in 1597 six people,
including Queen Elizabeth, a wealthy cloth merchant,
a scullery maid, two schoolboys, and an overworked
apprentice, attend London's Bartholomew's Fair and
come away with unforgettable experiences.

[1. Fairs—Fiction. 2. London (England)—History—
16th century—Fiction. 3. England—Fiction.]
I. Title.   PZ7.S875854Bar   1990
[Fic]—dc20   89-27230   CIP   AC

FOR TOM

CONTENTS

THE MORNING
OF THE FAIR

arly on a misty morning, on the twenty-fourth day of August, in the year 1597, the bells of London Town began to ring in clamorous harmony. The bells of Old Bailey and Stepney and Bow, of Fleetditch and Aldgate and Paul's. Chimes and carillons— the deep bass of St. Paul's, the bird-tongued treble of St. Mary-le-Bow, the clear cadence of St. Margaret's at Westminster—from parish to parish they swung in high steeples, casting a message, like a flock of birds let loose, through the thick, swirling fog.

Awake! Awake! Get up, get up! Bestir! It is morning!

The citizens heard and stirred. Among the thousands who opened their eyes to the morning, to the fog, to the

summons of the bells, were six folk of varying stations in
life who would foot it that day to Bartholomew Fair.

The Queen's Majesty herself, Elizabeth of England, and
a wealthy cloth merchant from the City would go to the
Fair because they wished to and none could say them nay.

The others were:

1. A scullery washmaid, one of the children who slaved in
   the palace kitchens at Whitehall.
2. A bright lad who studied Latin from dawn to dusk at
   Westminster School. Also his friend.
3. An overworked, underfed so-called apprentice to a
   stonemason.

These four would be obliged to use trickery or persua-
sion ere *they* could see the Fair.

One way and another, all six contrived to get there. All
but one got back that night.

In the palace at Whitehall the Queen's Majesty opened
her eyes in her curtained and canopied sleeping bower and
shouted to her lady-in-waiting, who lay on a low truckle
cot at the foot of the high and regal bedstead.

"Ho, Bettice!" The voice crashed into the lady-in-waiting's dream. "Bestir yourself! Tell me the weather is fine
for the Fair! Get up, get up, you lazy creature! Has the fire
been laid? I am not warm!"

As the royal bed was surrounded by draperies of crim-
son velvet and cloth of gold, the Queen could not see for
herself whether the day was fine or foggy. She slept on a
great mattress of goose down and beneath a counterpane of

the same, but the air felt damp and chill, and Elizabeth was old and a-cold.

Even in summer the royal palaces, with their stone floors, stone walls, lofty ceilings, were never warm.

Bettice, lady-in-waiting to the Queen's bedchamber for the month of August, blinked and smothered a yawn before drawing back the curtains surrounding the enormous bed, fixed her eyes on a spot above Her Majesty's head, and said, "There is some fog, My Lady." She nodded toward the huge hearth, where a blaze leaped eagerly. "But the fire is—"

"Fog?" The Queen was outraged. "You say FOG? This is the last day of Bartholomew Fair. I intend to attend with Lord Burghley and a single Yeoman of the Guard. I shall mingle with my people, who are made happy at a glimpse of me. They adore me. What's this talk of fog?"

Bettice, a lady-in-waiting who had been kept up late and wakened early by her restless monarch, shivered despite thick wool socks and a woolen shawl over her night shift. Ignoring the talk of fog, she said brightly, "So they do, Your Majesty. The citizens adore you. You are the heart and sunshine of England, the joy of all of us."

Strange, strange, thought Bettice, how this old woman still strikes her courtiers dumb with awe and love, how she keeps the devotion of the people of England. Could they see her now in her night robes—see how she is skinny, wrinkled, how she appears runty without the layers of adornment with which she faces the world— would the nobility still gladly kneel at her feet, bow from her presence backwards, swirl about her like moths at a sunbright flame? Would the citizens go mad, still, at the sight of her?

Bettice thought they would. Her Majesty's candle began to flicker but yet outmatched in brilliance of brain and authority anyone else in the land. She was, indeed, a matchless monarch. Unlike her father, Henry, who had ruled by terror and bloodshed, this Queen was obeyed not because she was brutal and powerful but because she was intelligent and powerful.

At times she made her twenty-eight ladies-in-waiting rebellious as they coped with her moods and caprices, her quick temper. She snapped at flattery like a dog at a mutton chop, treated the greatest nobles of the land like servants, and the citizens of England like children. But a sudden wry glance, a quick smile, and they were hers again. No one she could not beguile and enchant—this aged, wizened, regal woman.

Now she barked, "This talk of *fog*, Bettice. How much truth is there in it?"

From boredom now, not sleepiness, Bettice turned aside to smother another yawn. "Perhaps, Madam, the sun will shine upon us—that is, upon the Queen's Majesty—later on. In time for the Fair."

"It had better. Where is my breakfast? Am I a bird, to hunt my own breakfast?"

"No, Your Majesty. Yes, Your Majesty. It has just arrived, Your Majesty."

Into the vast chamber, hung with tapestries, where the fire in the great hearth had begun to warm the air, came Roger, Gentleman of the Bedchamber, carrying his rod of office. He made a deep bow, leg forward, moved a step toward the bed, bowed again, sweeping the floor with his plumed hat.

"I trust the Queen's Majesty passed a peaceful night?" he murmured.

"Trust what you like. Bettice here tells me there is fog this morning. I do not wish to go the Fair in a fog."

"It will burn off in good time, Your Grace."

"Humph. What do you know. Where is my breakfast?"

The Gentleman of the Bedchamber lifted a summoning hand and in marched the Steward of the Royal Washbasin. He approached the bedside humbly, knelt to present a golden ewer of warm water and a fluffy towel.

The Queen dabbled the tips of her long pale fingers, touched them to the towel, waved the steward away, and looked impatiently as the Usher in charge of breaking the Queen's fast entered, followed by three cooks who would take the blame should Her Majesty find something not to her taste. In the forty years of her reign the Queen had yet to find fault with a meal, but would have flown into a rage had the three cooks-to-take-the-blame not appeared.

She was mostly a gracious monarch and mostly well loved by her people, if not, at all times, by her courtiers. Still, she had a temper that fired up more easily as she advanced in years. It tossed powerful men about like twigs in the wind. Weak people dissolved in puffs, like dandelion clocks.

This morning she was affable.

After the cooks-to-take-the-blame came six pages bearing trays. There were always six trays at the royal breakfast. There always had been. It was said that the Queen's father, King Henry VIII, had gobbled every morsel on every tray and considered this first meal of the day a snack.

From pictures of him that hung in the Long Gallery of the palace, it seemed possible.

The first five pages offered:

1. Baconed herrings and smoked mackerel, garnished with watercress.
2. Oysters flavored with almonds, cloves, onion, and ginger, garnished with nasturtiums.
3. Rice boiled in almond milk with preserve of raisins, cinnamon, carrots, peaches, pumpkin, horseradish, fennel, and nutmeg.
4. Eels in quince jelly, surrounded by nutted cheese and roasted melon seeds.
5. Hedgehog in cream, with chestnuts.

As each tray was presented, the Queen leaned forward, studied the contents closely, then waved it along. On the sixth tray was a Venice goblet, banded with gold, containing watered wine. Also a slice of the whitest bread, a fig, and a chestnut.

Bettice watched wistfully as the pages departed with the five untouched breakfasts. Far down in the kitchens all that good food would be cleaned up by who-knew-who, but *not* by a famished lady-in-waiting, here in the royal bedchamber.

Until the Royal Personage, who cared little for food and never thought to think that someone else might be hungry, had eaten and was dressed for the day, Bettice would remain empty.

Getting Her Highness dressed for the day took hours.

There was the shedding of night robes, the commencement of donning the many day robes, now warming near the fire. Linen chemise, delicately knitted stockings, embroidered blouse with leg-o'-mutton lawn sleeves, skirt draped over the whalebone farthingale hoop, a velvet overskirt, huge pleated ruff studded with bugle beads and pearls, court shoes with high mosaic buckles.

There followed the selection of the day's wig, which might take an hour while the Queen debated between dark red, light red, or a red somewhere in between. After that, cosmetics to disguise the aging face. Ground alabaster to whiten the skin, carmine to redden the lips, egg white to gloss the cheeks. A disguise only in the mind of the Queen, who never saw the reality. There was not a mirror in any of her palaces. Bettice wasn't sure when they'd been banished. Before, in any case, she had been honored with this onerous position.

At the very last came the bejeweling of the entire royal self. The older she got, the more adornment the Queen required, and the longer it took to get her bedecked for the day.

Chains of gold, chains of pearl. Chains of garnet and topaz. Brooches crusty with rubies and diamonds, sapphires and emeralds. The gold and enamel emblem of St. George. Hailstorms of rings and bracelets, aglets and spangles, fringes and feathers and beads. The Royal Personage issued from her bedchamber each day aglitter like sunlight on water. It seemed to Bettice and the other ladies-in-waiting that a normal person could not stand or move for the weight of it all.

A Queen, of course, was not a normal person. Especially not *this* Queen.

Bettice sighed unheard and waited with folded hands as the Majesty of England ate bread by the crumbful, took tiny sips from the Venice goblet. The kneeling page held the tray on outstretched arms that betrayed not a quiver. Bettice, imaginative to the point of sometimes wondering how another person felt, thought what an effort it must be for so young a lad.

This boy, son of a nobleman, sent to Court to learn dextrous manners and form useful acquaintance, was no different from hundreds like himself; but he was here where she could see him, and he was desperately trying not to tremble. Bettice found herself worrying about him.

It was this unaristocratic quality in this aristocratic young woman that made her the Queen's favorite lady-in-waiting, though neither acknowledged it. While she chafed at the Queen's quicksilver temperament, quaked beneath the flashes of high temper—Her Majesty sometimes struck a servant or even a lady-in-waiting, sometimes hurled precious objects against a wall, sometimes shouted and cursed like a Thames ferryman—Bettice was not one of those who laughed behind the royal back.

"What an old trunk of vanity," Jane Wycombe had whispered, only last evening, watching Royalty simper at a young courtier's flattery. "Look at her, Bettice! She *believes* those lies he's shoveling into her ear. Flattery should be sipped like fine wine, not gulped like ale."

"You never thought that up yourself."

"No. I heard the Earl of Essex say it. Not in her hearing, of course."

"How do you know what *he's* saying?" Bettice asked, nodding toward the courtier.

"Oh, come! *Look* at the scene, will you? Him on his knees, fawning over her bony paw—"

"She has beautiful hands."

"Then it's all of beauty that's left to her. And there *he* is, like a drone trying to clamber his way to the Queen Bee's chamber, and her all 'la-la-la, Sir, tell me more!' She ought to *see* herself once, crooked old fool. . . ."

But since the Queen had banished mirrors, she could not see herself.

"That Queen Bee has a terrible sting," Bettice had snapped at Jane. "Keep on speaking so, and you're like to find yourself in Tower Yard without a head."

Even so, she rather understood the rash remarks. Jane and the knight in question were in love, but he'd caught the Queen's eye for a moment. If he wished to remain at Court—everyone wished to remain at Court—all he could do until she dismissed him was flatter and fawn and form outrageous compliments that the old Queen did seem to take as sterling.

What must it be like, Bettice wondered, to be old and ugly and losing your hold of the reins when once you'd been young and—well, probably the Queen had never been comely, not like Bettice herself, but anyway *young*, and the most powerful person in the kingdom, maybe in the world—what would it be like to find all that slipping away, and you with no way to stop time?

The most powerful woman in all the world, but, as Sir Walter Ralegh once said, "This is a lady whom Time has surprised."

Bettice, sympathetic in a shallow way, did not expect ever to be powerful. She did not expect, either, ever to be other than young and beautiful. Time would not surprise *her*.

But she was growing restless, watching Royalty's slow progress through that skimpy breakfast. Makes the eating of a chestnut last as long as a twenty-course meal, Bettice thought, closing her eyes to conceal the famished impatience in them. One did not show impatience in the presence of the Queen's Majesty.

It would be hours yet till she herself got a morsel to eat. Hours.

Far from the Queen's bedroom, far down in one of the vast palace kitchens, Merrycat, scullery washmaid to the root vegetable cook, stirred and shivered on her pallet of straw. She drew her smock of rough homespun over her knees to warm them.

Even in August the windowless kitchens, with their thick stone walls and hard-earth floors, were never warm, and Merrycat, youngest of the vegetable maids, did not have the privilege of sleeping near ovens or hearth. The geese that wandered in and out, whither they would, were luckier.

"Get up, get up, you lazy creatures!" said Agnes, the cook, going down the line of sleeping children, nudging them gently in the ribs with a wooden clog. She had a kindly nature and rarely mistreated the scullery boys and girls.

Merrycat stumbled to her feet, for which she had no clogs, awake at once, bright-faced, smiling. "Today is the last day of the Fair, Mistress," she chirped.

"And what's that to do with you, or aught of anyone here, including meself?"

"I just thought—maybe— Well, what I was thinking is—was—that if you—if we—that mayhap or maybe—" Merrycat drew a breath and said quickly, "*I was thinking we could go to the Fair!* Just for the tiniest while, Mistress," she added, as if this made her daft scheme reasonable.

Mouths open, the other children looked from cook to washmaid in silence. Merrycat, unlike the rest of them, never waited to speak until spoken to, and she did have the—the *sauciest* notions, being something dafty and so not responsible.

Bartholomew Fair!

Who but Merrycat would've thought even to *think* of the *idea* that any here, any of them, tatterdemalions of turnips, would be let *go to the Fair*!

"If you are *actually* thinking," said Agnes, her face red with astonishment, "that there's a chance that you'll be let go to the Fair, you've thinks in plenty to add to that." She waved her radish-carving knife. "You!" she said to Merrycat. "You go beyond yerself, and growing worse by the day, and it'll be getting you into trouble and not too far off, if you ask me."

Merrycat wasn't intimidated either by enormous Agnes or by her tiny vegetable knife.

"Wouldn't you like to see it, Mistress?" she coaxed. "There are stalls of pasties and pears and sweeties and gingerbread boys with gilt on them, there. And pipes and horns and—and *fiddles* to hear. And there's morris dancers and acrobats and a hobbyhorse man and a Gypsy to tell yer future. Wouldn't you like to see all that? Oh, don't you long yerself to be going this day to the Fair?"

The cook frowned hugely. "What do you know of fiddles and faddles and gingerbread boys, that've never in yer life been past the kitchen gardens since they scooped you out of the gutter and dumped you on me?"

"I hear things. I listen. Mistress!" the girl said, almost

rising on tiptoe and taking the others into her glance. "There are *toys* there for sale! Toys, Mistress! Dollies and poppets and whistles and rattles and tin soldiers and drums that people *buy* and give to their own children to *play* with!"

As drudges in the palace kitchens were orphans, waifs, strays that no one could account for, or children who had been turned out of their crowded homes and told not to come back, the notion of toys had not until this moment found room in their heads.

Toys! Things to *play* with that people bought and gave to children that they kept at home and maybe—maybe *cared* for. Even Merrycat, with her moony, cloud-shaped notions, did not use the word "love."

Like toys, love was nothing to do with them.

More and more seized with this particular cloud-shaped idea, Merrycat skipped about on her bare and dirty feet, scuffling straw in which old vegetable parings rotted and goose droppings collected. "Oh, Mistress, just to *think* of the Fair makes me dance inside. . . ."

"Poh. Poh, poh. Dance inside, is it?" She tapped her temple with one finger, looked at the others. "Loopy, poor thing. Now, Merrycat, you eat yer loaf end, and toss down yer cider, then dance yerself over to that barrel of beans and carrots before I clout you. The Fair, indeed! Such high jinks are not for the likes of you and me, as good as jailed in this kitchen."

"*Anyone* can go to the Fair, says Jack," Merrycat persisted.

"Jack, is it? Well, Jack can go stand in the corner and say what he likes, it won't stop the world from turning or get you or him to the Fair. There's an end on it." She rounded on the rest of the children. "The lot of you! Stir yer stumps before I lay into you broadsides! Jack, indeed. I'll give *him* what for." With her apron, she shooed several geese toward the door.

And there! In Jack came, staggering under a load of wood for the stoves and the hearth.

"What's this yer after telling poor foolish Merrycat here, that anyone can go to the Fair?" the cook shouted at him.

"Fact," said Jack with a grin. Cook didn't worry him, not one bit. "Let me tell you some'at—Her Majesty, her own Royal Queen Bess, herself personally is going this day to Bartholomew Fair, with His Loftiness Lord Burghley."

"And how come you to know that, pray? Her Majesty has taken to whispering into yer ear her plans for the day?"

"Bettice told Peter, the Usher, who told one of the tray bearers as they were coming down the stairs—"

Boxing Jack's ear, Agnes said sharply, "*Lady* Bettice and *Master* Peter. And I'd chop off that 'His Loftiness' afore yer overheard. People land in the Tower for talk like that."

"Me, Mistress? *That's* flattery, right enough. Waste Tower room on the likes o' me?"

"You give yerself airs, Jack, 'll land you in the stocks anyway, one of these days, and that Merrycat with you. Don't expect me to cry for you."

"Ah—it's all between ourselves, Mistress. A bit of palace gossip to stuff our heads with, there's little enough to stuff our bellies." He lifted his head, sniffing. "They've brought down the trays from the royal bedchamber. I can smell them from the breakfast kitchen clear to here. Get a

sniff of that, will yer? Oysters and cream and baconed herrings and the dear knows what all else and not a morsel for
us. Mistress Agnes, when'll you advance from root vegetables to the breakfast kitchen, taking Merrycat and meself
along?" He glanced about. "The rest of this rabble can stay
where it is."

The children, too cowed by the trio of talkers, did not
protest. Merrycat looked as if she might speak, then was
diverted by odors wafting toward them.

All of them—cook, wenches, and boys—swallowed
hard, their mouths watering at the thought of what was
being consumed in the kitchen next to theirs, though it
could be one of the thousand palace rooms above for all
that they could reach it.

This happened every day, after the hour of the Queen's
breakfast. The great meal of the afternoon, when twenty or
more courses were served and what was left over came
down to the kitchens beyond these, didn't trouble them so
much, as it was too far for odors to reach them.

Hunger they had always known, but the odor of food so
close was something they could not get accustomed to. It
would have astonished them to know that stories overhead, in the royal bedchamber, Bettice, the lady-in-waiting, felt faint with hunger she was obliged to conceal.
Bettice, of course, at some time during the day would get
to eat well. It would have left them trembling with dis-
belief to hear that the Queen, her own Royal Person, who
could eat anything she wished to eat, as much as she
wished to eat, who could eat all day long and no one to
stop her, *didn't care about food at all.*

There was no way they could have understood, or believed, so wild a story.

Now Agnes looked about with a tremendous scowl that sent them scurrying to work. Satisfied that they were decently occupied, she commenced carving radish roses, part of the garnish for dinner.

Jack shrugged, departed for more wood. Merrycat settled beside a barrel of beans and carrots and began to scrub.

As she worked, she thought about the Fair that was ending this day. Jack said it was all things you could imagine and a lot you never anyway could. *And* he had said that *anyone* could go. Once away from here, if you could find a way to get away, and if once away you could find your way to the Fair at all, none could bar you entrance to the grounds of Bartholomew Fair at Smithfield.

What was to keep her from sneaking out the kitchen door to the wicket in the gate that led from the kitchen gardens directly onto the street? Jack had told her of it and said it was never locked by day. She'd be off and away before they missed her. Among so many scullery children, maybe she'd never be missed at all. If, come evening, she could not get in again, what of that?

She was not sure how old she was, but surely had enough years to make her way in the world, somewhere and somehow. *After* she'd been to the Fair.

In Westminster School, in the lofty dormitory where the boarding scholars slept two in a bed, Jeremy Hensbowe opened his eyes as the bells of St. Margaret's began to ring, sweet and muffled, through the fog. He slid to his feet quietly so as not to awaken Jones Tarleton, who, as usual, had taken the whole blanket to himself during the night, wrapping himself in it so tightly that the only way to get part back would be to wake him up, something Jeremy would do only if the nights were much colder.

Jones stayed up late every night crying himself to sleep. He was afraid of the dark, afraid to go to sleep for fear of not waking up. He hated the school, his studies, the Headmaster, the Undermaster. All he wanted was to go home to his horses, especially to Captain, his own gallant steed, of which he talked constantly. It usually took the clang of the bell ringer right in the room to get him conscious in the morning. Still, no point in taking the chance that this day he'd wake on his own.

Jeremy tiptoed down the row of beds, occupants still asleep and some a-snore, toward the little room at the end of the hall where the Undermaster, Mr. Camden, spent his nights. William Camden was the finest teacher in all the land. And the kindest. And the most understanding. Sometimes, in a scholarly, classical, Latinish way, he was even jolly.

Still, Jeremy hesitated halfway down the long room and looked about, undecided. The dormitory had been a granary when Westminster was a monastery. Before Henry VIII, who'd been father to Queen Elizabeth, dissolved the monasteries altogether. There were a few narrow windows high in the cold stone walls. It was foggy outside, but with a hint of gray dawn. Soon the bell ringer would rouse with a terrible clangor the whole sleeping room.

So he had best decide to go forward with what he thought of as his Plan, or abandon it, or devise another way of following it. What gave him pause about going to Mr. Camden was that kind, understanding, and occasionally jolly as he was, it seemed unlikely that the Undermaster would agree to a design that had seemed so sensible, so *reasonable* the night before.

In the dark, with Jones sobbing beside him, Jeremy had formed this Plan. He would go to Mr. Camden, explaining how with Mr. Grant, Headmaster, away in the City, it would be a grand idea to let the boys go to Bartholomew Fair. If not all 120 of them, then Jeremy Hensbowe and Jones Tarleton alone.

In his mind he had held a conversation, taking first his own lines and then the Undermaster's. They would be speaking, of course, in Latin, as all in school were required to do except for one half hour at noon, when they ate, and after dark.

"Mr. Camden, Sir," his own part had begun, "it would be *good* for us to get out of school and to go to the Fair. Latin would come more easily, even to Jones, I warrant, if he had one foray past the gate." In what he considered a brilliant stroke, he'd added, "I think, Sir, it would be *instructive* for us."

"Enlighten me, Jeremy," the Mr. Camden in his head had asked, lips twitching in a way he had when amused but not prepared to show it. "Tell me—be precise now— how would instruction result from attendance at a rowdy, knockabout, thieving, cutpurse, riotous, uncontrolled, brawling bazaar like Bartholomew Fair?"

Jeremy thought he'd done a pretty job of presenting Mr. Camden's argument in Mr. Camden's very style.

"Why, Sir," he'd replied, "it will teach us the evils of being rowdy, knockabout, riotous, uncontrolled, brawling fellows. We'll be the wiser for witnessing such low behavior and no doubt will resolve to avoid such disorderly conduct ourselves."

So excellent a presentation it had seemed, so clever and disarming—in the dark, in his head.

So easy now, in the morning, to know how Mr. Camden would react. He might laugh. He might get cross. He might not reply at all. But this was certain: He would not for a moment consider letting anyone at all, much less the whole school, or even just Jeremy and Jones, go to Bartholomew Fair.

Turning on his heel, Jeremy went back to his bed, removed his nightgown, donned his dark knitted hose, blue woolen smock, soft leather boots . . . all the gift of the Crown. He sat, cap in hand, eyes on the floor, thinking what crazy notions a person could get in the dark, after a long day's Latin, with no relief in sight for years to come.

He did not himself feel a need to cry or even a longing to go home, though he often wished he were done with school. He was a Queen's Scholar—a "deserving poor boy" who'd been clever and lucky enough to secure one of the forty grammar school places for boys who were taught, clothed, fed, and housed by the Royal Purse. He was thankful that this bright chance had come his way and that so far he had deserved it.

Indeed, the year before he had been given a terrifying chance to prove his worth when Mr. Grant ordered him to compose a brief speech, in Latin, of welcome to the Queen's Majesty, who was coming to overlook her forty scholars next day and to hear them recite. To pen a speech was easy enough, but Jeremy could never remember afterward how he had got through the presentation, standing before the great Queen herself, stumbling, collecting himself, struggling on. He'd finished in a sweat of agony and shame.

And then! Oh, then!

She had beckoned to him, saying, "Come hither, boy. You shall have my hand, for a brave effort," holding toward him a thin white hand, heavy with jewelry. Jeremy had looked up, into the diamond-blue eyes that looked down into his with kindly approval. She nodded, ever so slightly, and he'd had the wit to lower his lips toward her fingers—not, of course, quite touching them and keeping his own hands behind his back.

He loved her. He would die for her. The greatest honor that would ever come to him was to be, by her grace and favor, a Queen's Scholar.

Nevertheless, he could understand why Jones Tarleton cried every night. Jones was a slow student, made slower by his fear of his father's expectations, fear of Mr. Edward Grant, the Headmaster. He was not able to study long hours, writing and speaking nothing but Latin, as was required, without falling asleep during the day. That, of course, meant flogging. Jones probably leaned over the three-legged flogging stool and submitted to the steady, rhythmic, stinging cane in the hand of Mr. Grant more often than the rest of the Westminster boys—the forty Queen's Scholars and eighty others—put together. Mr. Grant played no favorites; the sons of earls and dukes were chastised equally with lucky "deserving poor boys."

Unlike Jeremy's own parents, who could take him or leave him and had five sons and two girls besides, Lord and Lady Tarleton had only Jones. Lady Tarleton doted on her son. She would have kept him home had that been possible, but it was not. Lord Tarleton would have none of that, Jeremy knew. Jones would have, somehow, to plow his way through the years of Westminster, so that he could go to Cambridge or Oxford, so that he could one day become a proper Lord Tarleton himself.

Jones was not a popular fellow in the school. He behaved sometimes like a prince of the blood, rather than a mere future peer of the realm. This, though there were at school at least six boys who outranked him, the sons and grandsons of dukes. And Jones did snivel, did not take his floggings properly, without flinching. As he was forever boasting of the day when he would ride for the Queen in tournaments, outjousting all comers, this did make him rather the fool. Nevertheless, Jeremy felt protective toward him. He was so very unhappy and lonely, so dimly endowed in the head.

Jeremy sighed now. Oh, yes, he was sorry for Jones, and envious of him, too. What would it be like, to have a mother who would rather keep you home than send you to Westminster where ferocious Mr. Grant would stand you *in loco parentis* for year upon terrible year, trying to beat Latin into you? Did Lady Tarleton know how Jones was flogged because he could *not* construe Cicero? Wouldn't Jones, being Jones, have told her?

Probably not. She would, in turn, tell Lord Tarleton, who would fly into a rage, if Jones was to be believed, and why not? "A son of mine, whimpering at proper school discipline! I blush for you!" Jones would then be in for double floggings—at home and at school.

Jones said that his mother wept in the castle for lack of his company. They seemed a family easily moved to tears. Except the earl, of course.

No, the path was laid down for Jones. Westminster. then Cambridge or Oxford. *Then* a life of horses and the hunt. Why put a boy like Jones, who when he got through with schooling would never read a word again in his life, through the torment of learning how to? It was only with Jeremy's help that he was contriving to get through at all, and Jeremy sometimes wondered if it was harder for him to explain the rules of Latin grammar to Jones or harder for Jones to have them explained to him.

Here and there a boy stirred, blinked, yawned. Then, shattering sleep the length of the hall, came the *clang-clang-clang* of the bell ringer's waking signal.

With the Headmaster away, Jeremy thought they might have an easier time of it today. Mr. Camden understood when a fellow got so tired by late afternoon that he drooped into sleep with his head on the desk. It seemed to the boys of Westminster that Mr. Grant understood but two things—Latin and flogging.

Rich and poor, bright and slow, aristocrat or carpenter's son, all Westminster students came under the rule and rod of Mr. Edward Grant, who believed he could thrash into any boy lessons unlearnable from books or teaching. That Latin would not enter the head by way of a caned bottom did not concern Mr. Grant, who laid on till he drew blood, then demanded that a boy conjugate a verb, construe a sentence, translate a verse from Ovid's Latin to the Queen's English—none of which he'd been able to do before he got flogged. When still he could not, Mr. Grant fell to beating again.

Jeremy had been caned but once, when Mr. Grant had demanded of him the Latin of a word he'd never heard in English. "Thaumaturgics." How could a person put *that* into Latin? He'd made a brilliant escape from the second flogging by shouting desperately, "Sir, I believe the word to be Greek, so perhaps the Romans took it whole, so perhaps it just *translates* as 'thaumaturgics'!"

Mr. Grant clicked his teeth in a way he had and said, "Excellent, Jeremy. Excellent. Go to your seat." He had been to the faintest degree indulgent of Jeremy since the day of the Queen's visit. Feeling, Jeremy supposed, that I was a credit to him. *Which I was.*

"But what does the stupid word *mean*?" Jones and the others had asked later.

"Who knows? I don't. He didn't ask what it meant. He just said put it into Latin."

"How did you know it was Greek?"

"It sounded Greek."

Later he asked Mr. Camden, found that it meant "magic" and was, indeed, a Greek derivative. This kind of reasoning and curiosity had won Jeremy his Queen's Scholarship.

If your Latin flowed brookishly, the Headmaster found other reasons to lay on. The school day began at dawn and ended at dusk. Boys got tired. They grew restless, turned saucy or quarrelsome . . . behavior that brought a pupil under Mr. Grant's eye. Correction by the rod followed.

Rarely, but now and then, a boy went sobbing to Mr. Camden, who would pat him on the back, explain that this was how things were, had been, always would be, that others before had survived the ordeal of grammar school, as would others to come after, that there was nothing to do but stick it out for later rewards. A poor boy, by traveling the Latin road, would have a chance to rise in the world. A lad of wealth, like Jones, would be prepared to take his proper place in it—knowing something of the classics. The Queen wanted around her only classically educated courtiers, even if they'd forgotten anything they'd ever learned.

Now how, Jeremy wondered, not for a moment abandoning his intention, shall I bring this off? How get me and Jones to Bartholomew Fair? Between last night and his imaginary conversation with the Undermaster, and now at the start of the school day, his mind had made itself up. One way or the other way, they two would get out of here today and go footing it to the Fair.

He approached Mr. Camden's door and knocked softly.

In his great town house John Kempton, Esq., cloth merchant, turned fatly in his enormous bed, sat up, adjusted his nightcap, and waited for breakfast to be brought him. Across the room a lackey was laying a fire. It should have been laid earlier, but Mr. Kempton was not a man to scold. Fog swirled about the windows, an annoyance on this, the final day of the great Fair at Smithfield. Possibly it would burn off betimes.

Mr. Kempton would have liked to speculate to someone about the chances of the fog's dissipating in time to make the last day a crowning business success. It would have made him happy to indulge in modest bragging of the money he'd already made, selling his wools and velvets, his silks and brocades, his fine laces during the past three days. He yearned to speak with becoming reserve of the even finer prospects that lay before him. Possibly a knighthood sometime soon! Not blue blood alone brought knighthoods these days. Wealth brought it. Bought it. The Crown, always needful of stuffing for its coffers, looked kindly upon men like himself, able to lend, at good interest, large sums of money.

Mr. Kempton, who adored the Queen, was happy to lend. It was, of course, only good business to ask a proper interest.

He wanted to speak aloud of his rise in the world and to explain how he was sharing his good fortune, not *hogging* it all for himself. A charitable man, he did not wish to be acclaimed for giving. No, no, not that. What he wanted was for people to see that he was not a selfish man, that he had not forgotten, never tried to hide, his mean beginnings. No giving himself airs of one born to the purple or anything like. Just, in justice, letting his generosity be somewhat known. Who was there to heed or find interest in this facet of his nature?

He had no one even to talk about the weather with.

He looked across the room at the fire-laying lackey, whose name was—was—what the deuce was it? He called out, "What is your name, lad?" The boy whirled, ducked his head so that his chin was quite on his chest, and made no answer.

"Surely you *have* a name, child!" Mr. Kempton, who was almost deaf, spoke in a hearty, booming voice, convinced that other people could not hear unless he shouted. He was unaware that when he thought deeply or awaited the answer to a question, his lips tightened and his spiky eyebrows surged together over his nose in a manner that looked, to a beholder, wholly ferocious.

At the roaring voice and the false menace of Mr. Kempton's thoughtful frown, the boy hunched as if expecting a blow, so that the merchant sighed, saying, "It's all right. Run along now."

Life had made a coward of that lad. London was over-run with such starvelings, orphaned or discarded. They lived as they could, gathering rags to sell, thieving when possible, scouring ditches for table refuse, begging their bread. None was turned hungry from John Kempton's door. This boy had arrived when the butler said they were in need of an additional lackey. Here he was, months later, still creeping about fearfully, though he had kindly treat-ment under this roof.

Had kindness, or at any rate lenient handling, come too late to stiffen his backbone? Apparently that's it, thought Mr. Kempton, who'd been a brawling, burly boy himself and had thought to have such a son.

He had no son.

Looking around the room, he caressed with his eyes the tapestries hanging on his walls. The carpet, imported from Persia, that lay upon his floor. Downstairs, in the great hall where he entertained, the floors were strewn with rushes, as in most houses, even the proudest. If hearsay was correct, many of the great estates of the nobility made do with rushes. But he, John Kempton, had a Persian car-pet on his bedroom floor. He picked up the gold cup that gleamed on his bedside table, turned it around, put it back.

Tapestries! An Oriental carpet! Gold! A butler! A lackey—lackluster lackey, to be sure, poor thing—to light his fire!

This house-proud merchant had begun life herding sheep on his father's few and mingy acres. There he would be still had he been a man like his forebears, never lifting their eyes from the croft or dreaming beyond it. But the boy, John, as he sheared their scrawny flock, handled the coarse, dull yield, had envisioned long, lustrous, fine-fibered wools that would take prizes, command high prices. He had dreamed, too, of the life that would come of fine wool and high prices.

On stony hillsides, guarding sheep that even as lambs seemed without spirit, he dreamt of the world he wanted to enter, a world in which he was rich, respected, a member of the Clothworkers' Guild, able to read and write like a merchant prince.

Over his father's roars and curses, though it meant he never had more than three hours' sleep in a day's course, he attended the free grammar school in Lichfield, the town where he'd grown up. How proud he'd felt, fastening his first hornbook to his belt! How exultant to discover that letters and figures were not senseless scribbles but the key to the world!

He, son of an ignorant, unlettered farmer, had learned to read, to do figures, to write a fair hand!

When his father, stingy old hoarder, finally died, leaving not so meager a sum as he'd led his son to expect, John Kempton bought a fine ram and well-bred ewes to replace the cat-shanked creatures the old man had always settled for. He'd studied the market, learned to sell his good wool at a good profit. He'd gone from the dismal farm of his boyhood to a larger one, to the purchase of a mill, to the exporting and importing of other fabrics.

To put the matter plain, though he had no one to put it to, John Kempton had gone from strength to strength, from his miserable, hungry boyhood to this rich house, its carpet, its tapestries, its gold cup, its . . . *elegance.*

All his own work, and no one to speak to of it, brag to of it. No one to leave it to. No son, no daughter, not kith or kin. Except Herbert, who didn't care a whisker for anyone's riches or knighthoods. He had Herbert—Mr. Kempton smiled—and Herbert loved him for himself alone.

Long ago his wife had died. He didn't miss her. Since her going, he'd lived alone with Herbert and the servants. Hugely fat, rather homely, pretty deaf, and very shy, he'd not the courage to go courting again.

Just the same, and on the whole, his life suited him. True, it was a lonely one, despite his frequent and lavish hospitality. His many acquaintances accepted invitations to banquets given in his vast hall downstairs. They ate his food, drank his wine, passed an evening at cards, listened to musicians and actors hired specially for entertainment.

No one wanted to listen to *him*.

He did not take this personally. He was—besides fat, homely, almost deaf, and rather shy—realistic. It was his opinion that few people willingly listened to anyone else's triumphs, tragedies, or plain daily matters. That included himself. Didn't he, for the most part, attend another man's conversation just waiting for his chance to interrupt?

No, no—he was not discontent with his lot.

Today, for instance, he would go to Smithfield, where the Fair sprawled over many acres. First he would overlook his assistants, see that all was being properly done to move his rich goods along. Then he would stroll whither he would, taking in the sights—the freaks, the acrobats, the puppet shows, the minstrels. The pickpurses! Mr. Kempton quite enjoyed watching a skillful purse snatcher at work but guarded his own scrip closely. Come early afternoon, he would stop in a likely looking booth for roast pig and ale, then saunter on, this way and that, perhaps to the field where the archers and the tilters at the quintain showed their skill. That was always amusing. He would not come home till time to dress for the Clothworkers' Guild dinner at Westminster.

For the Fair, not the tidiest or cleanest of arenas, he would wear simple clothes. Small wig, a bloom-colored long coat, buckled shoes. Ah, but at tonight's dinner he planned to make a show in his brown periwig with curls to his shoulder, his new camlet suit with wide-skirted primrose yellow jacket, embroidered vest, white satin knee breeches, and tasseled leather boots. He would carry his gilt-handled sword, to which he was entitled. Very rich and fine he'd be.

Oh, it was a proud time when he mingled with men of substance, spoke with his fellow merchants of weighty matters—of the quality of Flanders wool, the price of Italian silk, the wondrous quantity of cloth of gold and cloth of silver required by the Court. To these men alone could he freely boast of great takings at the Fair, the only price being an ear in turn to their brags. Tonight, indeed, he would have as guests two important wool weavers from Flanders. He had met them on the opening day of the Fair, when they had purchased his entire year's wool clip, and on impulse—he was a man of impulse—invited them to the Clothworkers' dinner to which they, as foreigners, could not have entry. It pleased him mightily to be able to do this favor.

Always, at such functions, he reminded himself of the long way he'd come—from the leaky hut and lean pickings of his boyhood to this select company in the great Banqueting Hall of Westminster. Because he could not forget that hovel, the rags he had worn, the hunger pangs of his belly, Mr. Kempton had long since made an oath. Whatever he spent on himself for rich things—fine clothes, beautiful furnishings, new periwigs—he donated half as much of the cost to the poor. It made his mind easier to relish his luxury when all about him, all over London Town, he saw poverty and misery.

He had worked hard, but Fortune had dealt well with him, and he did not forget to thank her. He was well content—if he didn't think too far or reflect too deep. If he blunted the thorn of his loneliness with tapestries and carpets, goblets and gilt-handled swords, dinners with men of affluence. If he comforted the conscience that troubled him by offerings in the poor box, donations to Christ Hospital for Children.

If he averted his gaze from the children, the children . . . shivering in their rags, in their hunger, in their thousands.

He gazed at Herbert, stretched at the foot of the bed, lazily regarding him. They looked deep in each other's eyes, and Mr. Kempton thought they communicated.

"How now, Herbert!" he said. *"Tell* me true. Hold nothing back for fear I'll take offense, since you must know I can never take offense with you. Have I come so far in the world, with a chance to lie knighted in my tomb, with a coat of arms—my crest will be a black cat astride a ram on a field of azure—have I come this far with only you to leave the glory and the riches and the coat of arms to, that don't give a tinker's miaow for any of it?"

Herbert opened his mouth in a wide, pink, needle-toothed yawn of surpassing cleanliness, then walked up the rose silk coverlet and butted his great head against Mr. Kempton's ear, purring in what the merchant took to be a sympathetic manner. His nose was moist and cold as an icicle, his fur soft and warm.

Mr. Kempton, possibly one day Sir John, ran his hand down the cat's sleek back, to the tip of the powerful tail. Herbert's fur put him in mind of Italian silk velvet, of French satin, of the finest lawn from Bruges.

"You come of a tribe," he explained, as the cat closed its eyes, "that can keep its own counsel and needs no audience. But I—pity me, Herbert—am of a tribe, Herbert, that wants always to talk, to boast, bemoan ill luck, trumpet triumphs. Noise, noise, constant noise—that is the way of human beings. But you, Sir Fur, have made a servant of Silence."

Mr. Kempton babbled on to this creature he loved, a striped cat rescued as a kitten years before from a gang of villainous boys, intent on a death by stoning, for the amusement in it. They'd got him cornered when Mr. Kempton came along and saw in the skinny, snarling creature something brave and tough. In the way he'd looked about, seeking escape where there seemed none, prepared against all odds to fight his tormentors, to claw his way forward, the animal had reminded Mr. Kempton of himself.

A cat that would not give in, as he'd been a boy who would not give in.

"Here, you young scoundrels!" he'd shouted. "Leave off, or I'll have the lot of you in the pillory!"

The ruffians had laughed. Pillory for the stoning of a cat? A laughable threat. Altering policy, Mr. Kempton threw a handful of farthings in the air and, while the urchins scrambled and fought amongst themselves, whisked the little cat away and bore it home with him.

Now, here they were, older and fatter, a man who had everything and a cat that asked nothing but food and could get that on his own should the need arise. Cats stood on their four feet, asking no quarter. Herbert here beside him, courted and cosseted, fussed over and fondled, treated to the best of everything, needed nothing. Turned out of the house tomorrow, he'd make his way—resourceful, unresentful, unconcerned.

"Tell me, Herbert—as you have no use for wealth, and I shall have no use for mine when I depart this life—how to dispose of it?"

He rubbed his chin. Scratchy. He must get in the barber. He frowned, and thought, and said to himself that since the hour of a man's death was not to be predicted, he must apply himself to proper consideration of the disposal of his fortune. While without scruples about lending money to the Crown, so long as Queen Elizabeth wore it, he had no mind to die leaving all to some usurper, probably, who would come after her. One could wish her immortal, but she was not.

"Are you certain you'd have no use for a mansion and a pile of yellow gold?" he asked his cat, who curled next to him and went to sleep. "To charity then, since I've no one of mine own," murmured the merchant, leaning a little toward self-pity but bringing himself up short.

How *unbeholden* was a cat. Came with his own fur coat, his own weapons, his senses superior to a man's. Can hear what men cannot, see what men miss. It was said that cats could see through shadows. That was a strange thought. "Unfold to me, Herbert," said the merchant. "Is it true that you look through shadows? Will you peer through the veil of the future and tell what lies there for me?"

Increasingly aware of hunger, Mr. Kempton reached for

the bell rope to summon the breakfast page. What the deuce were they at in the kitchen, to keep him, *almost* Sir John, and Herbert, the best cat in London—neither of noble blood, but what of that—waiting this way? Had he been a different sort of man, the rod would be called for. But like William Camden at Westminster School, John Kempton did not believe in beating children.

In the year 1597 that was odd indeed.

Earliest of these six Fairgoers to be roused was Will Shaw, in the workshop of Peter Paston, stonemason, located on Seething Lane, in the parish of Westminster. Master Paston had, for helpers, one journeyman and a lad he had found shivering in the alley on a bitter, rainswept winter's eve and taken in and put to work. He called this boy his apprentice. Since even a guttersnipe must have a handle to be summoned by, he called him Will Shaw, the first easy one that came to mind.

"Mark you," he'd said severely that first day, "because of the goodness of my heart, you are now articled to me for seven years. Try running away, and I'll have you in the stocks."

Will, thankful to be out of the rain and the cold, pleased to have a name, unaware of his rights, unaware that there were such, put up no argument. He had been with Master Paston a full two years and, though overworked and underfed, continued grateful.

Peter Paston and his two helpers were presently engaged, under the direction of a far more successful master mason from Hartshorn Lane, in lengthening a series of brick walls in the Queen's Privy Gardens at Whitehall Palace. Will was happy there, surrounded by acres of greensward. He relished the sight and scent of thousands of roses, the air filled with birds singing, all of them flying about—so free, so free! He enjoyed the task that Peter Paston found mortifying—fitting the small peach-colored bricks neatly together with the thinnest layer of mortar to hold them.

Once, at a distance, the great Queen herself had appeared, walking very fast, so that the . . . courtiers, they were called . . . that crowded around her had to hurry to keep up; that looked pretty funny to Will, but of course, he'd not dared laugh. An old lady covered with tinsel and glass, mobbed about by people flapping their wings and their whiskers at her—so the Queen seemed to Will. It had much pleased him to watch the courtly procession, even so far off.

Master Paston and Burt Crumb took no pleasure in the green grass, the roses, the singing birds. They never lifted their heads from the task at hand, even to look at a Queen. Will, in two years, had not discovered them to take pleasure in anything or curious enough to look about at the world, either on Seething Lane or in the Queen's beautiful gardens.

It was not Peter Paston himself who kicked his apprentice awake of a morning, this joy falling to Burt Crumb, the short, barrel-built journeyman. Heavy-humored, heavy-handed, heavy-booted, he hated apprentices, masters, masons, bricklaying, all women, most men, and, since it could hardly be avoided, himself.

With this constant storm of ill temper brewing within, he was positively pleased to find Will Shaw still asleep on the straw in a corner of the workshop. Ample reason to kick the sluggard awake to the day's labors.

Will's teeth clamped together as the thick leather boot struck his ribs. He flung an arm across his face, since it was likely that Burt Crumb would follow the waking signal with a warning buffet on his ear, but he leaped to his feet without a sound. Small, skinny, usually tired, always hungry, Will was backed by a spine that yielded to no one.

"Grab yer loaf end and get out to the alley with you," Burt growled. "Load the wagon and mind how you do it. Yesterday you dropped a brick and cracked it, any more such carelessness and I'll—"

Have you in the stocks, Will said to himself with a shudder.

"Have you in the stocks!" Burt Crumb bellowed.

Will heard these words almost daily, and had not been, his personal self, yet in the stocks, but the thought frightened him. It was a sight common enough in London. Arms and feet and sometimes even the head of a person were locked in holes in a wooden frame, in marketplace or square. There they remained in the public gaze, pelted with garbage, jeered at, tormented, until the law saw fit to release them. It was horrible, and he did not intend to do anything that might land him there. Bad enough to be locked down in the cellar overnight, which Burt Crumb found reason to do often enough.

Will had heard from Mrs. Cartwright, who lived above, that at least two boys before him had run away from Master Paston's workshop, and he thought one day he would do so himself. But not yet. He remembered too well nights when he tried to coil upon himself for protection against rain and sleet and freezing cold. It was never, in his recollection, warm. Nor could he remember having even bread and lard to eat, though he must have done, or he'd not be here today. Sparrows required something in the belly, or they turned up their little clawed feet and died. So, too, did alley children.

No, he would take life here as long as he could, to learn the trade of mason, before he ran away. Take hunger, floggings, nights in the cellar—until he was ready.

They think it will fright you, Will, he would say to himself. He talked to himself constantly, for lack of another to heed him. They think, look you, that being left in the dark and the damp with the rats rustling and the spiders crawling around their great webs and the cold leaking in through the stones will make you shiver and stay awake the night long. That's what they think when they push you down there and leave you till morning comes and time for work and yer lucky those days to get a loaf end with a bit of lard at all.

That's what they thought, those two rough men who held his life in their thick-fingered hands.

They were right, though he would die of fright before he let them know. Released in the morning, he would saunter up to the workshop, stretching and yawning, as after a good night's sleep. Drove Burt Crumb mad, that did. Now, followed by more shouted instructions and warnings, Will snatched up his stale end of the loaf, smeared it with lard, and shot outdoors, into the fog and fracas of morning on Seething Lane.

This was a street of poor masons, of which Peter Paston was chief, having, besides his two helpers, a two-wheeled cart and a crooked-back old horse to haul his bricks. Other laborers on the short street carried their materials in hods, stumping beneath them, heavy laden, from workshop to work site, back and forth, from dawn to dark.

Though the wooden sign that creaked on chains above his shop declared Peter Paston to be a "master mason," he worked under, and at the pleasure of, the true master masons of Hartshorn Lane. He envied them bitterly, helplessly coveted their fine houses, their expert journeymen, articled apprentices, stout carts, sturdy horses. He was deeply, unceasingly jealous of their lordly choice of the best jobs in London. Envy spoiled his food, disturbed his sleep, soured his temper.

Daily, on the job, the master masons of Hartshorn Lane spread their plans wide on trestles, waving the likes of Peter Paston to one side, leaving him to stand dumbly by while vastly important consultations with famous architects were conducted in full view of all at the site. Peter Paston felt that Burt Crumb and Will Shaw eyed him with contempt as he waited, cap in hand, to be noticed, to be assigned a minor task somewhere on a wall, a mansion, a cathedral.

He was right about his journeyman. But for Burt Crumb master masons were no different from kings or cockroaches, all equally to be despised. He was wrong about Will, who didn't comprehend his master's lowly state. For Will, true master masons were as distant as royalty and nothing he had leave to think on, either to admire or to despise.

His job, and he was now busily at it, was to load bricks—as much as the horse, Casper, was able to drag— onto the two-wheeled cart, while dodging as best he could garbage and worse being thrown out of windows above.

Seething Lane was narrow. Its houses, with jutting upper stories so close that people could clasp hands across the street, were they so minded, seemed to lean together, and more than feather quilts and dusters were shaken at the windows, more than washing water tossed down to the street, regardless of passersby. It was said by a few old inhabitants that Puffing Dick, the King of the Beggars, had lived here for a while just before he was taken and hanged. Everyone on the street was proud to believe this, as Puffing Dick had been an exceedingly violent and dangerous character . . . the kind of man most admired in these parts. For his own part, Will thought beggary a sorry trade.

Life went on in a ceaseless din, this morning somewhat muffled by fog. Rakers shoved past him, sweeping up the night's garbage and offal. Workmen stumped along, carrying their hods, balancing lengths of lumber on their shoulders, hauling mortar in wheelbarrows. Women and children brushed past him, the women shouting at the children, the children yelling at one another. Beggars—children, old men and women, drunkards, cripples—scrounged in the long ditch that ran in the middle of the street or drifted through the alleys, looking for scraps of food, gathering discarded rags to make into bundles they might get a few pence for. Some, past any effort, huddled against the walls, staring or sleeping. No one paid them mind. Skinny dogs chased cats. Skinny cats chased rats. Skinny rats ran about in broad daylight.

Will found nothing here strange. This was how life was. Master Paston would always be there, vinegar-tongued, glum, giving orders in a thin voice that could barely be heard, but you'd better not miss any part or it'd go the worse with you at the hands of Burt Crumb.

And Burt Crumb!

Burt Crumb, far more than Peter Paston, was the central fact of Will Shaw's life, as much a part as hunger, as labor that knew no holidays, no fun, no play. For Will on this mean street, words like "holiday," "fun," "play" would be as foreign as the Latin he struggled with was to Jones Tarleton at Westminster School.

Carefully laying the bricks, one atop the other, in the rickety wagon, Will jumped beneath the eaves as a shower of garbage fell with a splash. He blinked in astonishment to see amidst the mess, a whole, an entire, a large and beautifully orange *carrot!*

Not glancing up, sure that whoever it was—Mistress Cartwright, he guessed—would immediately realize her accidental loss and come pelting down the steps after it, he seized the vegetable, rubbed it on his smock, broke it, and, while gobbling the one half in nervous haste, nipped around to offer the other half to Casper, who munched greedily. Will thought he saw a look of gratitude in the old eyes.

"Good fer you, young un."

Will whirled, half-expecting a cuff, though the hoarse voice was not harsh. It was—a marvel on this street—even cheery. There beside him stood a hugely tall man with a shining bald head. He had a sack on his back, and carried a contraption like a—a tall box with a window in it.

"Don't *tell* on us," Will whispered urgently. "About the carrot."

"Now, now. What d'ye take me for—a stravaging informer? A scurrilous gossip? A skulking confidential agent, purveyor of tales to the likes of that jumped-up journeyman that was ordering you about? The Caligula of Seething Lane, I take it."

"His name's not Caligula; it's Burt Crumb."

"A figure of speech, lad. A descriptive appellation. A metonymy or synecdoche—what you will."

Not troubling to puzzle out the words, Will recognized good humor as if he'd encountered it somewhere, somehow, long ago. But it amazed him to see a man who could smile! Heart ensnared, he tipped his head back and gazed, a long way up, into the stranger's eyes. Greatly daring, he said, "What is that, Master, that you're carrying? That box thing? And what is that in yer sack on yer back, too?"

"Curious, are you, eh? That's good, that's good. I don't know for sure that curiosity killed the cat, but it always improves the boy, no doubt of that. So, my lad, you want to be apprised of the significance of my box and the arcana of my baggage?"

Will, encountering a genial gaze in which there was nothing to fear, nodded, and the long man set his box down, and his sack, stretched his shoulders back to ease them.

"*This* is my puppet theater," he said, patting the frame of his box. "And in the sack, look you, are my puppets. Here, let me show you."

He took from the bag a dangling creature with a rag body dressed in red checks and a hard face with red-tipped beaklike nose and sharp chin almost meeting.

"This is Punch, my premier performer, as arrant a knave as ever you could shake a fist at." He shoved Punch back in the bag, whisked out a lady even uglier. "May I present you Judy, Punch's wife. Isn't she a beauty? Mind you don't marry the likes of *her*, though, to be sure, Punch is a wicked enough husband to turn a saint sour." Into the sack went Judy, and out came a small bundle wearing a fluffy cap. "Here we have their baby . . . poor thing, with such parentage it encounters many vexations, and how it survives is a wonder. They have a dog, too, in here somewhere . . . it bites them every chance it gets. And this— let's see, yes, here we have the Doctor . . . he's always having to attend the injuries Punch and Judy inflict on each other and anyone else in reach. And this fellow, look you, is the Devil himself, horrible looking, is he not? I have the devil's own work controlling *him*, let me tell you."

One after the other he removed the puppets, introduced them, popped them back in the sack. There was Jack Catch, the Hangman. Pretty Polly, who was, he said, Punch's girl friend, of whom Judy was furiously jealous. Then the Constable and his officer, both in uniform.

"And let me just see—Dagonet, the horse, is in here som'ewh—" The man was going on, his hand in the sack again when Burt Crumb burst through the workshop door with a look as ferocious as that on Punch's face, or even, Will thought, the Devil's.

"What do you think yer about, you lazy clod?" He grabbed Will by one ear and boxed the other. "I'll teach you to waste time gabbling with street vagabonds!"

"Here, here!" the stranger said in a grating voice altogether different from what he'd used to Will. "Unhand that child, you distempered ditch rat, you boorish churl, you servile bullying hog grubber—"

Burt Crumb's mouth fell open. Almost absentmindedly he let go of Will and turned his attention to this wordy clown who stretched up like a beanstalk almost to the first story of Peter Paston's house.

"Scarper!" he said. "Take yer rubbishy baggage and get moving, before I kick you down the street!"

"Pray, now—who do you think you are, to order a man of the theater about in this wise? Under what aegis do you presume to challenge me, Humphrey Mickle, puppet master, who have performed for the crowned heads of three conti—"

"I'm this stupid here's boss, that's who I am, and he's to get at his job. NOW! I don't care if you've performed for the crazed heads of Bedlam, if you don't pack up and be gone on yer own—and since yer built like a blooming maypole, I couldn't reach up to kick you—there's plenty here will help me to help you on yer way. . . . We don't care for stravagers on this street!"

"Sure of assistance, are you?" said the puppet man, looking about at a considerable crowd gathered near to form an amused audience. No one moved to help Burt Crumb to help the man of the theater on his way.

Will, who knew that he was going to pay hard for this deviation from duty, looked at the stranger pleadingly. "Master, I have to pile bricks now. I—it was fun—thank you fer—but now I have to—"

"Get cracking!" Burt Crumb shouted. He added in a low voice, "I'll see you on this matter later, never fear." He glared at the puppet man, scowled around at the crowd, stumped back into the workshop.

Will, with much to fear at the journeyman's hands, ducked his head and began to pick up bricks as Mrs. Cartwright, who'd been hanging out her window to watch the goings-on, now came hurtling downstairs to run up and down the ditch, bewailing the loss of her vegetable.

"I threw a carrot down here! It was quite by accident! It should be returned to me, by honest folk!" she cried out. "It was my only carrot! It was to go in the soup with a bit of onion and a morsel of fowl! And now it's gone! Has anybody seen my carrot?"

This appeal was met with silence, and the crowd began to disperse. Will, not looking at Mrs. Cartwright, piled brick upon brick in the cart but kept an eye on Humphrey Mickle, who, having shouldered his sack and his theater, was preparing to move on.

"Lad," he whispered, "I'm off to Smithfield, to entertain the Fairgoers. If you think to come also, look for me by Kip-the-Pigman's stall; it's the best place to gather a crowd—"

Catching sight of the journeyman looming in the doorway, he turned his back, reached into his sack, spun about, holding Punch aloft. The puppet, no longer a slack-bodied doll but a living, wicked-looking rascal, waved his arms about and said in a shrill, carrying voice, for all to hear, "Farewell, then, boy! Do your duty by that slack-jawed, boar-eyed, ham-handed, squint-eyed, ditch-begotten villain there. . . ."

A shout of laughter went up as Burt Crumb started forward in a rage, then halted when he found his face square in the puppeteer's chest, and retreated, scowling.

Off went Humphrey Mickle, tall as a maypole or beanstalk. Will aligned bricks, wondering whether Burt Crumb's form of penance would be bad enough to erase the joy of this encounter with the puppet man. He didn't think so. The journeyman had not, to Will's way of thinking, brains enough to think up new punishments, and he was used to all the old ones.

Casper whinnied dismally. Mrs. Cartwright sought her carrot up and down the ditch. Children cried, dogs howled, rakers raked, and presently Peter Paston slumped out of the workshop and said wearily, "All right, you two. Let's get started. I suppose this cursed fog will continue the day long."

No one knowing him would have supposed him to suppose anything else. His eyes were always firmly fixed on the gloomiest corner of life.

With Peter Paston leading—or, rather, dragging—Casper, Burt Crumb and Will Shaw following, they set off for Whitehall. Only Will, of the three, would take pleasure in the minor but absorbing job of lengthening a wall in the Queen's Privy Gardens because only he was entranced by the vast greensward, the thousands of roses, the flying and singing birds, and the chance of a glimpse of the Queen.

A half hour later, as they passed through the arch of the palace gate and began to walk down the King's Road to the gardens, they heard neighing and the heavy thud of hooves of war-horses, the clatter of lances on shields in the Tilt Yard. Courtiers were playing at battle. This Queen had so kept the peace during her long reign that to *play* at war was the closest her knights could get to it.

The King's Road was over a mile long, leading past the Tilt Yard and Banqueting Hall, past the Privy Gardens, Westminster Hall, St. Margaret's Church, Westminster Abbey, and so, at the very end, to Westminster School.

Once, working on the garden wall, Will had seen a file of schoolboys pass. He'd sat back on his heels for a moment to watch them, quizzing himself. Now tell me, Will, what do you think it'd be like—to go to school, learn letters, wear hose, have boots to yer feet, a blue smock without a rip or stain, instead of this canvas you've on yer back and never had another? Wouldn't you strut about like a rooster? Wouldn't you be the cock of Seething Lane in yer finery and yer learning—

Burt Crumb had clouted him back to work.

GOING TO
THE FAIR

he sun was out, and a frisky, fragrant breeze blew from the Queen's Privy Gardens as Jeremy Hensbowe and Jones Tarleton walked down the King's Road toward Whitehall Gate.

Jones stared about, openmouthed, in a dazed and dazzled fashion. Was he—were they—really *out* of the school, *away* from the schoolroom? Was he, in truth, breathing the air of the world outside? Was that wheel of rooks croaking and turning over the Abbey real, or were they dream birds? Not letting Jeremy see, he pinched his thigh. He felt it, but maybe you'd feel a pinch in your sleep? Was he—were they—*in truth* released from loathsome Latin for the entire morning? Or was it still night, and he having the nicest, kindest, foolishest dream of his life?

"Well, Jones?" Jeremy said, giving a happy hop. "Why don't you say something? Aren't you going to tell me how marvelous I am? *I* find myself *extraordinary*."

"But how did you do it, Jeremy? I don't understand how you got Mr. Camden to let us *do* this. Three whole hours free to do what we want—"

"Not to do what we want, Jones. That is, we *will* be doing what we want, which is to go to the Fair. But we aren't free to do anything else. That's the bargain I struck. Half an hour's walk each way, two hours at the Fair, back to school."

"But *how*? What did you *say*?"

"Word for word a conversation I made up last night while you were sniveling—"

"I was *not*—"

"Of course you were. You always do. Maybe I don't blame you, the way you miss home. In any case, this morning we—Mr. Camden and I—had this talk where I said what I'd planned to say last night, and he just about gave me the answers I made up for him." He shook his head in wonderment. "It *is* hard to believe. I told him about the *instructive* benefits that would accrue from a visit to the Fair—"

"Instructive?" Jones, who was not entirely slow-witted, wrinkled his nose, and his mouth turned down wryly. "You *are* a fair trickster, Jeremy."

Rightly taking this for a compliment, Jeremy said, "Actually and in fact, we both knew that was so much twiddle-twaddle, but I explained how you are in such a bad way, bawling practically all night and too sleepy and dull next day to get much past *amo-amas-amat*—"

"Hold now!" Jones said imperiously. "Guard your tongue there!"

Jeremy pulled off his cap, swept it to the ground in a low bow. "Yes, Your Lordship. Grant a poor misspoken scholar pardon, Your Lordship. Shall I kiss Your Lordship's peerage's practically *royal* foot—"

"Oh—stop it, Jeremy. But I'm not stupid. That is, not in every way, all the way through—"

"I didn't say you were."

"You might as well have." Jones walked a few yards in silence. "I am not, you know. I don't have the kind of mind to construe Horace or Virgil, but I could construe a horse better than any of you."

"How construe a horse?"

Jones, with a triumphant air, said, "It just means 'explain,' doesn't it? 'Understand and interpret'? Well, the horse isn't born that I can't understand and explain."

"Well said!" Jeremy shouted. "Well said, Jones!"

For a moment Jones Tarleton pinkened with pleasure, but thinking about horses—the finest of God's creatures— then realizing how long it would be before he could go home for a few days even to *see* a good mount, he drooped again.

Clever Jeremy had struck a bargain with the Undermaster, but only for two hours, with another to go to Smithfield and get back. To strike a bargain with a schoolmaster, even one so usually lenient as Mr. Camden, was beyond Jones's understanding. Schoolmasters imprisoned boys. They beat boys, made sport of them. Spoiled their days, ruined their nights. Ruined their *lives.* It was what schoolmasters were for, not to give boys leave to go footing it to a Fair. Yet here they were, he and Jeremy, on their way without hindrance. But only two hours, and one to come and go!

"Could you not have made it the whole day?" he said crossly.

"Well, lawks and lord-a-mercy, listen at that! A minute past, you were calling it *three whole hours.*"

Jones, pondering, didn't reply. It had crossed his mind that now, away from the jailers of Westminster Grammar School, he could escape altogether. He thought he would know the way home, if he could find a carriage or something to take him there. Mr. Camden had allowed him to take a few shillings, for him and Jeremy to spend at the Fair on something to eat. Jeremy hadn't a farthing, being a poor person, a mere carpenter's son, a Queen's Scholar, getting his education and keep at Crown expense. A good companion, of course. Jones would never deny that.

I could *walk,* he thought. It would take days, and there'd be people come after, trying to find him, hunt him down. But if he went by footpaths and byways, and not by highways. If he traveled at night and hid out by day—

"Mind," said Jeremy, reading his friend's thoughts, as he always seemed able to do in a most annoying way, "we have given our parole to return in two hours. Our honor is involved."

A pox on honor, thought Jones. There was too much talk of that in school. They spoke of honor at home on his father's estates as if it were more important than anything else. More important than wealth, or horses, or happiness. Men lost everything for honor, died for it. Women suffered in its name. Boys were sacrificed, sent from home to horrible schools, to be schooled in honor *and* Latin. Jones hated both.

To the bad place with honor, thought Jones Tarleton, a free person whose every step took him farther from that prison, that dungeon, that pillory from which there was no release—that school. Well, there was this three-hour release that Jeremy had contrived for them, the dear knew how. And when the two hours at the Fair were up, *then* he'd decide whether honor or happiness was more important to him.

Jeremy was saying now, "Mr. Camden suggested we continue to converse in Latin, even if we *are* out of class." Jones turned and looked him in the eye. "I don't think he thought we'd take the suggestion."

"If he did, he's a fool."

"Mr. Camden's not a fool."

But Jeremy, uneasily guessing at his friend's thoughts, wondered if in this instance Mr. Camden had not been foolish. Maybe, he thought, I should not have got us into this. Maybe I and Mr. Camden are going to be very, very sorry. He shuddered, thinking of Mr. Grant's retribution on the poor Undermaster, on himself, on the entire school body if Jones here, instead of returning to school in the required time, just took off for home.

Oh, but he wouldn't, Jeremy said to himself, trying to feel reassured. Jones would not do that to Mr. Camden. To me. It would not be honorable. And Jones is an honorable person. He *is*, is he not? How would honor weigh in the scales with his longing for home and horses? Jeremy's step grew less light as they neared the Gate.

As they went past the high walls of the Privy Gardens,

a dirty boy without shoes or hose ran past them, then slowed, head turned slightly as if to overhear their conversation.

The future Lord Tarleton took offense. "Tell that lowsel to go about his business," he instructed the Queen's Scholar. "I'll not have eavesdropping."

Jeremy laughed, sweeping a hand heavenward. "Eavesdrop beneath the wide welkin, Jones? Skydrop, more likely, would you not say? Clouddrop, mayhap? Except there are no clouds. Now, that's an interes—"

"Jeremy! That guttersnipe is trying to overhear us!"

"Therefore you must stop telling me *arcana imperii*. State secrets," he added, at Jones's testy glance.

"Have a care how you jest with me, Jeremy!"

"Of course, Your Lordship." Jeremy swept off his cap again, made another low bow. "I forgot my place for the moment, Your Lordship."

"Oh, stop fooling. But I do *not* care to have a private conversation overheard by a—a lowsel."

"Jones, you're a snob."

"And you, I wot, a carpenter's son."

They stood, facing off, for a good few minutes. Then Jeremy turned and started back down the King's Road.

"Hold!" Jones shouted. "What are you doing? Where are you going? Come back this minute!"

Jeremy kept walking.

After a moment's hesitation Jones ran after and grabbed Jeremy's sleeve. "I'm sorry! I'm an ungrateful wretch, a miserable excuse for a friend. Truly, I am *sorry*— Please, please! We *can't* miss this chance at Bartholomew Fair. I won't be able to stand it if we don't go . . . and after you were so clever persuading Mr. Cam—"

"Enough, Jones. After all, you are *quite* correct. There stand you, son of the great Earl of Tarleton, and here am I, oh, alas and alack, a mere carpenter's fourth or fifth son—I forget which—who was so fortunate as to gain a Queen's Scholarship and have this grand opportunity to better myself in the high company of sprouting lords like yourself—"

Jones fetched a huge sigh. "Oh aye. You're going to punish me. I deserve it."

Jeremy laughed and threw his arm around the other's shoulder. "No. That would be meanspirited. I never mean to be meanspirited. Large in all ways, that's my ambition. I intend to be like Mr. Camden, the biggest-souled, kindest-hearted, decentest man in England."

They continued toward the Gate, past the Tilt Yard, where the usual war games sounded. Thunder of galloping chargers, clashing of armor, yells of challenge and triumph, bellows and grunts and groans. Peers of the realm and princes of the blood playing at battle! Just to hear them filled Jones with heady elation.

One day *he* would ride into the lists, a paladin astride his great war-horse. He and his steed would be armored in black and gold, like the Earl of Essex. His shield would be embellished with the quartered arms of the Earls of Tarleton. He'd have a great plume to his helmet, an escort of twenty or thirty squires, wearing his livery, in attendance. Perhaps he'd allow Jeremy to be among them. He would drop his visor, level his thirty-foot lance, and CHARGE down the line. . . .

Oh, to break a lance in the Tilt Yard! *There*, indeed, would he honor Honor. There! Only there!

With a whoop of defiance, he pelted away from Jeremy, down the King's Road, then wheeled and raced back, arm out, stiff and steady before him . . . his invincible lance. Shouting the name of England's most famous tilter, the Queen's Champion, he yelled, "Have at thee, Sir Henry Lee! 'Ware my lance!"

Jeremy ducked in time to avoid being struck in the eye, came up scowling, and they walked on without speaking, Jeremy increasingly uncertain of the wisdom of this foray, Jones allowing to himself that in real battle, as in the tourney, Honor came before all else.

But this Queen, despite the triumphant defeat of the mighty Spanish Armada, was set against even little wars. He had many times heard the nobles in his father's castle grumble at her petticoat rule, harking back to the long-past days of King Harry.

"*There* was a man who joyed in the flow of blood," an earl had said at table one night. "No matter how shed, or by whom," spoke up another. "He misliked it mightily to be his own, if memory serves," said the Earl of Tarleton, and the rest of the company laughed.

Preoccupied with their own musings, neither boy now paid heed to Will Shaw, who followed at a distance.

In a short time they heard the clatter of approaching hooves and jumped aside as a light carriage, red and gold and royally crested, sped by. Regarding the coachman in green silk livery, the two beautiful, beribboned, shining black horses, the Yeoman of the Guard in scarlet jerkin standing at the rear of the carriage, they swept off their caps.

"*Vivat Regina!*" Jeremy shouted.

"Long live the Queen!" Jones called, with an irritable glance at Jeremy, who had determined at least to introduce a word of Latin now and then this day.

Facing the coachman, taking up the seat with her wide skirts, was the Queen's Majesty herself, bedizened like a pirate's treasure chest.

"Did she nod to us?" said Jones. "I think she smiled upon me! My father is well known at Court. I'm quite sure she recognized me. Perhaps even you."

"Perhaps," said Jeremy, thinking it was good the Queen would not concern herself about why two schoolboys were wandering about in the middle of the morning so far from their lessons.

Will had found it interesting, and sort of comforting, to find that nobs fell out with each other like the brawlers in Seething Lane. Those two had been on the edge of fisticuffs before the big one, who was nice, laughed and put his·arm around the other, who was not, in Will's opinion, so nice.

Their talk was meaningless to him. In his world a carpenter's son and an earl's were equally to be considered nobs, and he'd have doffed his cap to either. What had seized his imagination was mention of Bartholomew Fair. There Humphrey Mickle was to set up his puppet theater next to Kip-the-Pigman's stall, so as to draw a crowd. And there he had said Will Shaw could find him.

Will drew a deep breath, blew it out, bit his lip, and talked to himself. You're supposed to run fast as you can, look you, Will, to the workshop to get a trowel to take the place of the one that the handle fell off of—and it wasn't your fault, Will, but he boxed your ears anyway—and bring back the new one he says you'll find behind the sacks of sand that are in back of the stacks of bricks and get back in a hurry or he'll have you, Will, in the—

He broke off, stopped walking, stared at a flock of rooks turning and turning in a great wheel over the Banqueting Hall and the Tilt Yard. If, instead of fetching the trowel, he took himself off to Bartholomew Fair, he'd be thrashed when he got back as never before and probably locked in the cellar every night from now on. And maybe this time they really *would* put him in the stocks.

Shifting from foot to foot, he weighed the price.

When a spanking carriage went by, with a coachman in front and a soldier or something riding behind and three tremendously fancy people sitting within, he pulled off his cap and fell to his knees on the cobbles. He had never seen her this close before, but *this* was the Queen. This old lady taking up a whole seat while the other two people squashed together facing her, this old lady covered with clothes and jewels till you hardly could see her, *this old woman was the Queen of all England.* And he, Will Shaw, had beholden her! Not, as beforetimes, far away in orchard or garden, but so near that the breeze of her passage whiffed in his face . . .

He heard the schoolboys, who were far down the road, shout, "God save the Queen!" He, too, shouted a blessing upon her. Master Paston and Burt Crumb would not believe this. If he told them. If he saw them again.

Would he see Burt or Master Paston or the workshop again if, instead of fetching the trowel as bidden, he went seeking Humphrey Mickle at the Fair? And if he did not see them, what matter? Could life be worse than he found it now? Well, mayhap it could. Where would he find his bit of bread and lard, his cup of cider, if not at Master Paston's? Where would he sleep o' nights? How would he finish apprenticeship to a trade that he'd already put in two years at? Even dirty straw in a workshop corner was a bed of sorts. Turned out, he'd be back in the alleys, roofless, supperless, without a way to earn his living. No one would hire a truant apprentice. He'd be back scrounging for scraps. Nothing left but his name. Will Shaw. He'd keep that.

What to do, what to do . . .

Puzzling over this hard decision, Will watched as the glittering carriage clip-clopped through the great Gate of Whitehall and disappeared. Those schoolboys were almost at the Gate, too, and would presently disappear. Knowing he'd already made up his mind, he ran after them. He'd never find Smithfield and the Fair by himself.

At the moment that the two schoolboys, with the mason's helper trailing, passed through Whitehall Gate, Merrycat slipped through the wicket of a lesser gate, opening on the Strand, at the end of the kitchen garden. Jack, clearly not believing she'd do it, had told her how to find the Fair.

"Walk straight north for a couple of miles, and then there'll be all sorts of folk and beasts headed in the same direction. You just join up with them," he'd said, grinning.

"What's north?"

Jack pointed. "That way. Keep the sun on your right hand."

"Which is my right hand?"

"You have two hands, stupid. One on each side." He'd touched her wrist lightly. "*This* is your left hand."

"So this other one is my right?"

"That's the only one you have left, isn't it?"

"Left? You said *right*."

"Pay heed, you silly. If the hand on this side is your left hand, the one that's left on the other side has to be the right hand, doesn't it? You really should not, you know, go anywhere by yourself. You aren't bright enough to keep out of trouble."

"Lots of people get to go to the Fair. Why should not I?"

"I just *said*. Your wits are addled. You'll get lost or maybe abducted by scoundrels—"

"Why would scoundrels abduct me?"

"They have their dark reasons," Jack said, then, giving her a funny look, added, "I guess *you'd* be safe from them. Who'd want—" He broke off, waved a hand toward Agnes. "But think, Merrycat! *She* maybe won't let you back if once you go off. Maybe she would be so angry that you can't ever come home—"

"And maybe I don't care a whiffle, so."

She was surprised that Jack, always acting so cocky, so even brave, was frighted at the thought of losing the "home" of this kitchen. Anyway, she did not think that Agnes would either be angry or refuse to let her back in.

Oh, she was joyed to find herself the brave and cocky one. Besides, whatever Jack thought, she was not a stupid. She was *fanciful*. She'd heard that word spoken by one of the ladies-in-waiting and taken it to herself. Fanciful. Whenever Agnes called her a lackwit, or Jack said she was a stupid, to herself she said, I am a fanciful, and the words warmed her.

Now, waiting until the cook's attention was elsewhere, she skipped out the door and ran like a hare down the long path to the gate, grabbing a handful of young broad beans as she went, and so through the wicket.

As she emerged onto the street and started north—or anyway, she hoped it was the direction Jack had pointed in, he'd got her all confused with that talk about her hands and the sun—she beheld the most wondrous sight of her life. Eyes blurred with astonishment, mouth agape, bare toes twisting in the dust, she stared as a carriage, gloriously gold and scarlet and filled with people who glowed like fire, sped past, throwing up a few pebbles, and was gone.

Trembling, Merrycat looked after it, saying to herself, They'll never believe me when I tell them in the kitchen that I saw the Queen! I saw the Queen's own very self go past in a fairy coach.

She almost turned back, almost gave up thoughts of Bartholomew Fair. What was a Fair, compared with what she had just beholden? She wanted to *tell* them. Agnes and the kitchen children who worked in the palace, none of *them* had seen this sight. Only she, the silly, the stupid, had *seen the Queen!* It had not been fancy. It had been her very self, the Queen that they prepared vegetables for all the days of their lives.

In a moment she stumbled forward. Who knew what else the day might bring forth that had begun with this marvel?

Earlier, in the vast cobbled courtyard of Whitehall Palace, William Cecil, Lord Burghley, the Queen's Secretary of State, had waited with folded lips, narrowed eyes, and tapping foot for the arrival of the Queen's Majesty, who had been seized by another of her notional schemes—this time to attend, almost without escort, the Fair at Smithfield. To mingle with her subjects. To prove again—

to whom? for what reason?—how she, their most glorious and gracious prince, was beloved by her people. How the sight of her was the light of their eyes.

During her long reign she had made a habit of this manner of foray among Londoners and countryfolk, often on horseback, sometimes a-foot. Gloriously gowned, bejeweled in Oriental splendor, nobly condescending, great Elizabeth—matchless among monarchs—this Queen who had made her subjects her only children, had appeared, over the years, in their wildly cheering midst, to accolades of love and loyalty.

But, thought Lord Burghley, nervously pacing, like all children, they grow restive under a rule that seems without end.

And like a mother, she *will not know this.*

Once a foreign ambassador had written, "The City of London is a stage whereon is shewn the wonderful spectacle of a noble hearted princess towards her most loving people, and the people's exceeding comfort in beholding so worthy a sovereign. . . ."

That had been long ago, over three decades in the past. The Queen was old now. Her grip on the reins of power, the affection of her subjects, slackened. Slightly, it was true. But noticeably. And now, when she was most in need of them, the great councillors who might have reasoned with her were lost in death. Except for himself, and his son, Robert, who was left to counsel this Queen, who would not submit to Time, to Time's changes . . . either in herself or in the temper of the people?

There was no one.

He felt himself growing old very fast, urged toward death by the whims of this capricious sovereign, this wor-

shiped and difficult Queen. Could Robert, who had tremendous intelligence and almost no tact, take up the
burden of service to Queen and State when the day came
that he himself was not here to lift it?

Which day, thanks to such escapades as the present,
was surely not far off. He thought of the words from St.
John 9:4: ". . . the night cometh, when no man can work."
At times he longed for that night, for the peace of it, for its
eyeless, unechoing, unending silence. . . .

Meanwhile, here was this preposterous equipage, sent
by the Earl of Essex, for what was supposed to be a simple
trip to Smithfield.

Gloomily he surveyed the crowded courtyard. Awaiting
Her Majesty was the royal pageant coach, big as a barge,
with twelve matched grays, plumed, belled, beribboned,
caparisoned. Four grooms in green silk livery and white
wigs, monarchial coat of arms woven in gold on their
sleeves, stood one at each corner of the carriage. Lord
Burghley marveled at how motionless they were able to
remain for hours, eyes so steady they looked painted onto
their faces. A host of equerries was present, the hooves of
their mounts clattering over the cobbles. Fifty scarlet-
robed Yeomen of the Guard held gilt halberds at stiff attention.

All this the doing of Essex, Master of the Horse, current
favorite of the Queen, called, by the unkind or the envious, "the plaything of her dotage." A peacocking gallant
of long lineage and short sight, insolently confident of his
sway with Her Majesty. As usual he'd ordered too much of
everything, to draw attention to himself.

The Queen had said she wished to go in modest array,
only himself, a lady-in-waiting, and one Guardsman for es-

cort, and here was this—this *elaboration* that would surely put her out of temper.

Had this Master of the Horse considered how they were to take this enormous coach *into* the grounds of the Fair, crowded to suffocation with booths and stalls, with vendors, entertainers, cattle pens, and mobs of citizens? When it became clear how preposterous, how wholly impossible was the undertaking, the royal wrath would be aroused.

Who would feel the whip of Her Majesty's aging rage? Not the Earl of Essex. Criticize *him* at your peril, said the Secretary to himself. No, no—look no further, Burghley, than your own nose. You, the man closest to, most trusted by Her Majesty since she'd come to the throne thirty and more years ago, will be the victim. During those long decades, she and he had moved yoked in almost perfect rhythm. She had heaped on his head honor upon honor, endowed him with wealth and estates so vast he scarce could reckon them up.

Nonetheless, the bolt of her anger would be shot right at his head.

He was smothered, pressed by the weight of his duties, the magnificence of his position. His rope had been woven of purest gold, but he was very nearly at the end of it. He was *tired*, and could not understand, never had been able to understand, why the woman he served seemed incapable of fatigue. She wearied, wore out, all around her.

"*Exhausts* us," Lord Burghley muttered to himself. "All of us."

Nonetheless, he took comfort in knowing that the Earl of Essex would one day go too far. That the Queen was deeply indulgent of him, all the Court knew. But he was a reckless, a feckless, a heedless, unthinking fellow who would not understand that England and her Crown were first in Elizabeth's heart. No mere man, however handsome, however dashing, however beloved, could alter that simple truth. In cruder terms, Essex was stupid and would one day pay for it. Of that Lord Burghley had no doubts at all.

Came a fanfare of trumpets, a cry of *"Way for the Queen's Most Excellent Majesty!"* and here she came. And in a rage. Here was England's great Queen striding toward him across the courtyard in a spangle of bright raiment and gems, crackling with fury, followed by a running lady-in-waiting, radiating despair.

"William!" the Queen shouted, when still many yards away. "What is the meaning of all this? Is my every command to be flouted? I did not order a cavalcade! Expressly, I said *simple*! I said a modest visit, *without* flourish, amongst my people at their annual cloth fair. This—this elaboration would suit a progress to the Earl of Leicester at Kenilworth!"

With half a smile at her use of his own word—it was as if in these thirty-four years of his service and her command they had grown together in their thinking—William Cecil sighed. She'd forgot, again, that Robert Dudley, her dearly loved Leicester, was dead a decade since, that she would never again set forth in pomp and panoply to visit him at Kenilworth Castle.

Increasingly the armor of the royal mind betrayed chinks. It was his task to seal them up, to make the Court and the world and the Queen herself believe that mind to be formidably armored as ever.

"Mr. Secretary, I liketh this not!" she said, coming up

against him, staring upward into his eyes, her own flinty with anger.

"I like it little myself, Madam. It was not I—" he began, and broke off. The first councillor to the Majesty of England did not put the onus, however deserved, on others. "If Your Majesty will, perhaps, walk in the orchard, I will assay to reason with her Master of the Horse—"

"Assay? What means this *assay*! Tell the Earl of Essex that he oversteps himself. Clear all this out—" She waved a hand at the great gilded coach, the grooms, the mounted equerries, the Guardsmen. "Get a small, open carriage—"

"Open, Your Grace?"

"*Open*, William. I'll have no barrier between me and my subjects today. Two horses, without caparison." Glancing at the Yeomen of the Guard, she added, "Keep that tallest one. He can ride behind."

Lord Burghley eyed the enormous farthingales worn by the Queen and Bettice Coyne. They would fill a small carriage and overflow it. To say naught of just where would he put himself, with skirts crowding every inch of space? Was he to ride behind, hanging on, like the Yeoman of the Guard?

"I beg leave to point out, Your Grace, that even a smaller equipage will be too large to drive through the cluttered grounds of the Fair. There simply will not be room for it."

"I do not mean, my Lord, to *drive* through. Did I not make clear my intention to *walk* amongst my people, lay my hands upon them, meet their eyes with mine? I desire to be *amongst* my citizen Londoners. To be one of them, their simple servant."

Simple servant, Burghley said to himself wearily, but

knew she spoke in earnest. Sighing, he summoned a hovering steward, instructed him to race to the stables and there inform the Master of the Horse, should he be there, and, if not, anyone he could lay hold of, to get a reasonably small, not too small, open carriage with two horses uncaparisoned and to have such equipage here with the greatest possible haste.

At that, he thought, relieved to find that Her Majesty had taken a notion to stroll toward her gardens, this little tempest was nothing to what would have resulted in her father's time. The faintest tinge of contrariety to *his* wishes and heads adorned the pikes of London Bridge within the hour.

Well, leave him to history. His daughter Elizabeth was clemency enthroned, by compare.

When at length a much smaller equipage arrived, the Queen had to be summoned from the orchards, where she was wandering with Bettice. She voiced no rebuke as she and the maid disposed their enormous skirts on the carriage seats. Lord Burghley, trying to make his bulk small, squeezed in beside Bettice. The tall Yeoman of the Guard mounted the step at the back; the straight-backed coachman clucked at the pair of simply adorned horses—scarlet plumes, ribbons in tails and manes, harness threaded with silver. Nothing elaborate.

Off they clattered, along the King's Road, toward the Gate of Whitehall, and so to Bartholomew Fair.

As they passed the wall of the Tilt Yard, sounds of clashing armor and heavily thudding hooves were heard, together with the shouts of the tilters.

"At their games again, are they?" said Her Majesty. "Fools! Rattlebrained sprouts of useless nobles! By His

Eyelids, I'm minded of children with paper shields and wooden lances. Ah, well, William—anything to keep them busy and out of trouble, eh? Let them play at war, not go to it," she added, laughing heartily. Her companions, as a matter of course, courtesy, and common sense, shared in her mirth.

They noticed three awe-smitten children by the road-side as they noticed hedges or bushes. That was to say, noticed them not at all.

John Kempton, in wide-skirted embroidered coat, gray breeches, and buckled shoes, without sword or periwig— he was saving those for the Clothworkers' dinner— stepped into the carriage he rented for his personal use. When he was able to put armorial bearings on the doors, *then* he would have his own carriage, matched horses, and all the delicious accoutrements that went with the possession of one's private equipage. Meanwhile, this handsome outfit served him well, and served no one else.

"To Smithfield," he directed the coachman in his usual trumpeting tone. "And how are you this day, Terence?"

"The length and breadth of me spine, Sor, is one long ache, and that's all on it."

"I'm sorry to hear that."

"Not so sorry as I am, Sor. But *there,* poor folk must endure."

"So, for that matter, Terence, must rich. When it comes to the revenge the body takes upon us as we progress."

"True, true. Still—" The coachman broke off. Even with so easy-humored a man as Mr. John Kempton, a fellow could go too far. Besides, what did *he* know of aches or pains, him and his grand house, his fancy clotheses, his ordering of people about? "To the Fair!" says he to me, and I do as he bids or lose his trade. What do the likes of him know of the poor?

I know what he means, Mr. Kempton thought. It is easier to endure pain in a feather bed than on a pallet of straw. I've known both ways. But what to say? Nothing. Words never cured a backache. He would give Terence a shilling over the day's hire, for what help that would provide.

Terence clucked to his horse. "The Fair again today, is it, Sor?"

"The last day. I must wind up my business and then take an hour or so to go about and see the sights I've been too busy to take in. You might like to do likewise, Terence? Here's an extra shilling you could spend."

"Now, that's a handsome offer, Sor, and I won't say no to the shilling; but if it's all one to you, I'll use it for family purposes."

"Of course, of course."

Leaning back as they jolted along the dusty, rutted road, John Kempton thought about Life. He pondered on how unequally its gifts were portioned out. He was far more fortunate than Terence, who, backache and all, was more happily situated than average Londoners, most of whom led lives of monotonous misery—poor, wretchedly housed, if housed at all, undernourished. Without hope. Terence here owned his own equipage to rent out, and that not cheaply. But Terence, to Mr. Kempton's knowledge, compared his lot only with those who had more than he, not less. As he himself did the opposite.

"Will you ever," he muttered, almost aloud, "take

proper pleasure in what you have and stop this constant care over what others have not?" He contributed heavily to charity. *Let him who has much give to him who has little.* That was what Scripture said, or something like it. Mr. Kempton was an indifferent churchgoer, but practiced what he did not hear preached. Still, he was never wholly pleased. Discontent when he was poor, discontent now that he was not. "You are a fair trial to satisfy, John Kempton," he told himself.

Not that he didn't relish the possession of his house, his sword, his carpets from the East. Not that he looked forward the less to taking his Flemish guests to the Clothworkers' dinner tonight, where they'd be in the company of other successful merchants. But always this—this *thorn* lodged in his mind, his bosom. He'd earned his wealth but never felt entitled to it. Not entirely.

Irritated with himself for being unable to accept without question his own good fortune—achieved through his own labor—he watched passing pedestrians. They looked, most of them, afflicted with concerns, with bodily pains, with sorrows that no one else cared about. Did they hate him, riding past in what must seem great state, indifferent to their suffering? And what could he do to make anything better, anything different?

He scarce could stick his head out the window and bellow abroad, "I care about all of you! I tell you, I care! I suffer for you!" They'd not believe him. Sneer, probably. Why should they credit the words of one who rode in style whilst they walked, many without shoes—

All at once he leaned forward, frowning in his unconsciously forbidding manner, and said, "Halt, Terence."

A grubby, undersized child sat by the roadside, rubbing

bare feet, staring about with an expression at once lost, frightened, and defiant. He looked up, startled, as Mr. Kempton's shouted "What are you doing there, lad?" came from the carriage.

Making as if to run, then sinking down again, the urchin put his head on his arms, turning it from side to side, as if shaking off the question.

"Here, here now. This won't do," said John Kempton. "Terence, I'll get out for a moment and inquire into the problem."

"It's just another street starveling, Sor. No need to trouble yerself about it."

Reflecting on the quality of mercy and how unequally it, too, was portioned out, Mr. Kempton squatted beside the child, who could not be cold on such a day, so must be shivering from some other cause.

"Are you lost, lad?" he asked in his penetrating voice.

A shake of the head, then a fairly vigorous nod as Will looked up to meet a most horrible frown. Accustomed to scowling looks, he met this without flinching.

"Will you tell me, where do you live?"

"No."

"Well, that's all right. Where are you headed?"

The lips turned in, as if to prevent information from escaping, then unfolded. "I were going to the Fair, Master. Only I lost them as I was following. Don't know the way now, or back either." The suggestion of a smile tucked the corners of the boy's mouth. "Guess I am lost." He stood. "I'll be going, then. Thank you, Master."

"For what?"

A hesitation, then a full, frank smile. "Fer asking after me vexations, Master."

"Vexations, is it? Now, there's a grand word."

"It was Mr. Mickle as used it. He has a power of words, does Mr. Mickle." The boy's own words came now in a rush.

"And who is Mr. Mickle?"

"The puppet man. I—that's why I was trying to find the Fair. To find Mr. Mickle, by Kip-the-Pigman's stall. Where he said he was to be found. Mr. Mickle."

"And who are you? That is—if you don't mind giving me your name."

"Won't give it. Tell it, though. Will Shaw, Master."

"I am John Kempton, cloth merchant. Well, then, Will Shaw, we might as well ride together, since I, too, am headed for the Fair."

"Ride in that there gig? Me?"

"Any reason why not?"

Tongue caught between his teeth, Will considered a long moment, then turned up his hands. "Thank you, Master."

To the snorting disapproval of Terence—the ruffian didn't even act humble—Will leaped into the carriage, and the trip to Smithfield resumed, Will Shaw stiffly upright, only his eyes moving from side to side in amazement, and no little resentment. This gentleman, with the fierce face and loud voice, was, he saw, a kindly gentleman, but should not go about hauling people into carriages. That he should not.

Meanwhile, John Kempton, comfortable now that he was helping somebody, glanced covertly at the lad, sitting so straight, rigid, and silent. The grimy hands were tightly locked; the slight frame seemed to show all its bones; the countenance had the pale, sharp-nosed look of constant hunger.

When we arrive, the merchant said to himself, the first thing—the very first—will be to fill that empty belly. Then we'll have a fine time, he and I, seeing the Fair in each other's company. I shall buy him a toy. A drum? Yes, a drum would be the very thing. Unless, possibly, a set of toy soldiers? Well . . . he shall have them all, and anything else he wants, Mr. Kempton thought happily as they jogged toward the Fair.

AT THE FAIR

n black sugarloaf hats, wide breeches, and short scarlet jerkins, the brothers Vetterer, wealthy wool weavers from Flanders, who had come to Bartholomew Fair to buy and sell, were spending the third day in idleness, taking in the sights and sounds. Tonight they would attend, at the invitation of the English cloth merchant John Kempton, whose excellent wool clip they had purchased, the Clothworkers' dinner at Westminster Banqueting Hall.

"We are fortunate, Nils," said the first gentleman, "that there is no rain. The climate of England is no improvement on our own, about which I forbear to speak. I was fully expecting storms before the Fair was over."

When it rained, the Fairgrounds of Smithfield became a

muddy frog pond, through which, nonetheless, Londoners and visitors from other lands plunged and elbowed in search of food, merriment, strange sights, bargains in cloth, in apparel, in wine, in entertainment. No downpour closed Bartholomew Fair.

Today was dusty underfoot, cloudless overhead. The vast acres were crowded with stalls, booths, tents and tables, cattle and sheep enclosures. The lusty coaxing cries and calls of costermongers, balladeers, ropedancers, jugglers, acrobats, morris dancers, trained animals jostled the air, mingling with conversations, arguments, quarrels, happy greetings, the laughter or tears of children, the bawling and bleating of beasts.

"Well, well, brother, do not lose heart. It may yet rain before the day is out," Nils, the second gentleman, said cheerfully to Jan, who took his pleasures sadly. "Let us walk about to observe the human folly, but first I shall have one of those luscious, juicy, plump-to-bursting pears."

"Let us hope the eating proves equal to the appearance," said the first gentleman, not sounding hopeful.

"What d'ye lack? What will you buy?" cried a costermonger of fruit. She stood, plumb and proud, behind pyramids of apricots, pears, plums, figs, and melons. They glistened with a light sprinkle of water, glowed in their colors like piles of gemstones, and were fully equal in the eating to their appearance. "Buy any pears, plums, apricocks! Very fine, very fine! Swelled with sweet juices!"

A few feet along—the stalls were close-crowded—another voice competed. "Oranges from Spain, from Spain! Over the main from sunny Spain! Draw near, draw near—

my oranges are very tempting! Come close, good people, and feast your eyes, delight your tongue!"

"Globes of sun-embraced beauty," said Nils, who grew lovesick at the sound of the word "sun." There was, as Jan so often pointed out, little of sunlight in Flanders. Or, he thought now, in England, for the most part. However, after beginning drenched in mist, the day was fine. For that one must be thankful. Nils took his pleasures gladly.

Now he studied the Spanish oranges as if they bore a message for him. Some, thickly studded with cloves, had been made into pomander balls. Their heavy, spicy fragrance obscured less wholesome odors rising from underfoot. The Vetterer brothers bought one each of these, fastening them to their belts, and each an orange, which they ate on the spot, letting the peels drop to the ground with other, less savory leavings of a three-day Fair.

"The gingerbread also looks tasty," said Nils to his brother, eyeing a display of little cookie men, ornate with gilt, on the ginger cake woman's tray. "I shall have one!" he declared. "Better yet, I shall have two!" He suited the action to the words, while Jan, ignoring the scowl of the fruit seller, pressed a pear at the stem end, prodded the plums, at length took an apricot with an air of resignation.

They walked along, eating and talking.

A toyman held up, one after the other, his poppets with grinning faces, his wooden soldiers jointed to dance on sticks, his cotton animals stuffed to plumpness, his leering hobbyhorses, his gaudy dolls and painted drums.

"Gentlemen! Ladies! Halt a moment and look at what I have! Here are toys for your babies, your precious babies! Soldiers for your sons, dollies for your dollies! I have rattles and drums! I have *whistles*—willow whistles! Hobbyhorses, hobbyhorses! Do you lack hobbyhorses? I can supply! Who'll leave the Fair without something for the children?"

The gentlemen from Flanders were apparently content to go home without something for their children. They strolled on.

Here was a man selling mousetraps. There a ballad maker offered to compose a verse on the spot, suitable to any occasion. "Fardels for farthings!" he cried. Would you have an ode to your lady love? He'd spit one out for a tuppence. A dirge for the departed? "A moment, Sir, while I grow grim."

Farther along, an artist undertook, for a pence, to limn a likeness to a sitter's satisfaction.

"Jan! Why do you not sit to this fellow? You've a handsome face for an artist to deal with. I doubt not he could omit the dyspeptic look altogether."

"Pray tell, Nils—who would want a likeness of me?"

"Why—your good wife, I am sure, would treasure—"

"Nonsense."

They walked on and presently, to their surprise, encountered Mr. John Kempton, who greeted them with his customary roar. His was a voice that caused passersby to turn in astonishment.

"Well!" exclaimed Nils Vetterer. "Well, well, well . . . what a happy encounter!" He and Mr. Kempton vigorously shook hands, smiling broadly. Even Jan looked not displeased.

"Where are you heading?" Nils inquired.

"Not to say *heading* anywhere. Just taking in the sights."

"We, too. One must grant the sights to be manifold and bemusing. Shall we join forces?"

"By all means," bellowed the cloth merchant to the wool merchants. "It would be my pleasure to have your company this morning as well as this evening." He looked around, in seeming perplexity.

"Is aught troubling you, Squire Kempton?" asked Nils.

"No. No, I suppose not. That is, I gave a child, a nice boy, underfed, a ride here in my carriage. I'd thought to buy him some'at to eat, but he hopped out when we got here and disappeared like a mouse in the wainscot."

"Shocking!" said Jan. It was unclear whether he meant that Mr. Kempton had given such a boy a ride or that the boy had sped off in such fashion. "With nary a thank-you. That's what come of indulging beggars—"

"Oh no! He thanked me, over and over, as we rode here. And didn't beg of me. Not a farthing. He simply scooted. Mayhap I overwhelmed the poor lad," Mr. Kempton shouted.

Nils smiling, Jan scowling, John Kempton frowning, they continued their walk.

A strolling corn cutter, displaying ominously rusty tools, cried assurance that he would painlessly pumice bunions, tweak out corns, clip toenails, even hair: "Most reasonably, good people, most reasonably, look no further!"

Mr. Kempton and his friends, who employed their own barbers and corn cutters, sauntered on.

Girls and women carrying mops or milk pails, young men and old with spades, shepherds' crooks, shoemakers' awls headed for the corner of the field where the Mop Fair was held. There they would stand in silence, holding aloft the emblems of their crafts or trades or simple abilities, hoping for hire.

Here was a striped tent. Within, according to the motley-suited, horn-voiced fellow in front, were to be seen "freaks such as your worthies have never laid eyes upon before . . . monsters that have thrilled and horrified thousands from the deserts of Egypt to our own green dales and shires! Step in, step in! For a petty farthing—what's a farthing to gentlemen such as *you* be?" he said, aiming his eyes at the three merchants. "You will find amazement, you will be astounded, you will be—"

"Once," Mr. Kempton said, "I put down my farthing and entered in hopes of amazement."

"Did you find your hopes realized?" asked Jan.

"I found a two-headed chicken, one of whose heads was sewn on, a three-legged chicken apparently genuine, a three-legged calf who had had the misfortune to lose a limb, and a creature yclept 'dragon.'"

"Prithee, unfold!" said Nils Vetterer, sounding amused. He himself put no credence in dragons, fairy gold, necromancy, or suchlike drolleries. "What manner of dragon met your astounded gaze?"

"On close inspection it proved to be a small pig encased in snakeskin with a horn fastened to its head. I bought it."

"You *bought* it!" Jan exclaimed.

"Oh yes. The poor thing was suffering. I cannot bear to see suffering if in some way I can relieve it."

Jan continued to look confounded at the behavior of this Englishman. "Did you eat it, then?" he asked. That, at least, would make sense of the pig business, though what could be made of taking a street urchin into one's carriage,

Jan was at a loss to explain. Not, he admitted to himself, that Squire Kempton appeared to feel explanation necessary. The English were a puzzling nation. John Kempton, he began to think, was odder than most. One could appreciate an invitation to the Clothworkers' dinner and yet recognize facts.

"I had no appetite for that," Mr. Kempton was saying. "After effecting its rescue, you understand. I gave it to my butler, and doubt not that the pig was eaten, but at least I took no part. One way or another the animal was out of its misery."

"In my view," said Jan Vetterer, "these"—he gestured toward the freak tent—"hoaxsters should be criminally charged as duping and cheating the public."

"In mine," said his brother, "I say that having acted like a two-legged, one-headed simpleton, one gets, for a farthing, exactly what's coming—for a farthing."

"For my part," said Mr. Kempton, "it is not the duping of the public that vexes me, but the wicked treatment of poor beasts that cannot protect themselves."

Nils Vetterer, a man of his century, found this sentiment extreme. He himself went to bearbaitings, though not frequently. The sight of savage dogs worrying chained and blindfolded bears was entertaining enough but quickly grew boring. He preferred a wrestling match, where sweaty brutes bashed each other around, giving men of finer feeling a sense of participation. He doubted if Squire Kempton here had ever attended a bearbait, a cockfight, a wrestling match. An overnice person, for all his enormous size and ear-shattering voice, thought the Fleming with perplexed tolerance. Apparently much given to doing "good." No doubt a genuine instinct, but smacked of the pompous.

Unaware that the Flemish merchants were summing up his character in this wise, Mr. Kempton was now observing, with considerable interest, a purse snatcher at work. How deftly, with what silent stealth, the fellow practiced his art. A horn thimble to his thumb so as not to be cut by the small sharp knife he employed, a speedy slice, and off in a trice in the crowd.

"Remarkable, quite quite remarkable," said Mr. Kempton. "I imagine it takes training. I doubt my fingers could achieve such nimbleness, even with training. Doubtless one should not admire a thief, but I have always an impulse to applaud anyone doing his job well."

"Still," Jan said dryly, "let us keep firm hands on our own purses, to forestall nearer admiration to this art."

On. A pause to watch tumblers fly through the air in cartwheeling, leapfrogging patterns so swift the eye could scarce follow. Then, still more astonishing, a man performing acrobatic feats on a rope stretched between two trees, at least twelve feet above the ground. Holding a goblet of water, he turned three somersaults without spilling a drop.

"One wonders how he does that," said Jan, skeptical even as he saw the feat performed.

"Last year," said John Kempton, "they had monkeys."

"Monkeys? Doing what?"

"That." Mr. Kempton gestured upward. "Four monkeys, and they had baskets of eggs that not one spilled out of when they went head over heels. It's a marvel, what can be done on a rope. I should think even more difficult than learning to cut purses."

He would have lingered to watch the ropedancer but sensed impatience in the other two. Why, if they purposed to *see* the Fair, this haste to have done with each spectacle? Might as well gallop through on horseback, he thought, a bit irritably for him.

Here, at a curtained booth, was a thin, sloe-eyed Gypsy woman, a glass ball on a small table before her. She provided a stool opposite, for those who would risk a glimpse into the future. On a shelf behind her was all manner of charms, philters, amulets designed to bring about desired results and intercept the objectionable.

"What asses there be in this world," said Jan, "to put credence in fooleries such as these."

Mr. Kempton's hand in his pocket closed on a walnut shell bound with gold thread, within which was a small dead spider. The Greeks themselves had held this to be a charm to ward off the ague, and in his case it was surely effective, since he had never had the ague in his life. As to *prognostications*—he pursed his lips. He did not, of course, credit such nonsense, but it might be interesting to see if by *chance* the seer had some augury concerning his knighthood. . . .

He looked from the corner of his eyes at his companions, who strode past the Gypsy's booth with an air of distaste. Even Nils, who seemed a fellow game for a lark, was contemptuous.

Avoiding the Gypsy's dark, inviting glance, ashamed to find in himself a remnant of peasantlike superstition, John Kempton moved along with his two acquaintances, still wondering where the starveling lad had got to in such a hurry. He had seen, in Will Shaw, something of Herbert, something of himself—all three sturdily defiant of life's monstrous odds. He and Herbert had won out, and in some nook of his mind surely the notion had been that he, in turn, could give this lad a nudge forward.

Well, well. No profit in further concern. The boy was gone, lost, absorbed in the crowds by now. Overcome by the carriage ride so unexpectedly offered? By the carriage itself? By—Mr. Kempton quizzed himself—by me *myself*? It crossed his mind from time to time that his great size, his deep voice might—just possibly—intimidate those who had no understanding of his naturally gentle humor. See how the fire-laying lad this morning had taken fright at a question kindly intended. . . .

Long ago his wife had said, after one of his sudden gestures of charity, that he did not *offer* his help, he *forced* it upon people. A kernel of truth there? Since attaining wealth, he had been unable not to rush to the aid even of those who had not asked. Perhaps he gave it—forced it—when help was unwelcome? That would be bad, very bad. Could he get the better of this disposition? If it was his nature to rush upon people and creatures with assistance, whether or not it was required, even if it was resented and he too blunt-witted to sense resentment, even if he played the *fool*—was there aught to do about that? A man's nature wasn't to be altered at this stage of life.

Well, so be it. He'd rather be a fool than a suspicious, ungiving man like Jan Vetterer.

He was beginning to get the impression, from these two merchants of Flanders, that they found him more *comical* than intimidating or well-intentioned. Could this be? If so, did he mind what they thought? He considered, concluded that he did not. He was as he was, they were as they were, and he had to know people a good deal better, value them far more, before they could wound his feelings.

He did begin to wish he'd not invited them to the Clothworkers' dinner. Still, when it was over, they would part,
doubtless not to meet again.

Nils Vetterer lifted his head, sniffed like a hound on
the scent. "What's this I detect perfuming the air? What is
this fine and savory odor wafting toward us? My stomach
calls out at the scent! Roast pig and mulled ale, i' faith! I
find myself possessed with a craving for roast pig and
mulled ale—"

John Kempton, mouth watering, recalled that the boy
Will Shaw had said he was searching for a—a Mr. Mickle,
puppet man, to be found near Kip-the-Pigman's stall. Perhaps after all, he could find and treat the young rascal,
who would surely not be able to buy himself a morsel.
And if I judge rightly, he told himself, there's too much
pride for begging in that bony breast. I shall need to be
subtle, if I find him.

"By all means," he said, stepping briskly forward. "Let
us find the stall of Kip-the-Pigman, who sells, I am told,
the juiciest pork, the finest of ales—"

But now there came a rustling, excited stir in the
crowd, a low humming that rose in volume till shouts of
acclamation rang on all sides, from every part of the Fair-
ground.

"*The Queen! The Queen comes! Make way for
Gloriana, Our Most Gracious Sovereign!*

"'*Way for the Queen's Most Excellent Majesty!*"

"*God save Yer Grace! Give you long life!*"

"*The Queen! The Queen! 'Way for Her Most Gracious
Majesty, Queen Bess!*"

Sweeping through shoals of citizens, who fell back, fell
to their knees, swept off their caps, wept, shrieked,

fainted, shouted approval of this utterly unexpected, wholly astonishing, magnificently regal act of condescension, the Majesty of England came striding, Lord Burghley at one side, Bettice Coyne at the other, the tall Yeoman of the Guard, halberd upright, marching behind. Her Majesty's alabaster features were aglow. Lord Burghley looked troubled, Lady Bettice sullen. The Yeoman of the Guard lacked expression altogether.

On they came, the Queen smiling, bowing from side to side, tripping along on her Court heels, farthingale swinging, jewels flashing. She sniffed a pomander. Over it her dark eyes flirted with her people. She was lively as a girl.

"Can it be?" said Nils Vetterer in a shocked voice. "On *foot*? Can that be the Queen, her very self? Surely not!"

"This passes credence!" Jan declared. "It's a mummer, surely. A vulgar imposture!"

He was confident that once this royal-seeming figure bedecked in tinsel ornaments had passed, a message would be found printed on its back, for the edification of those who could read. It would proffer the location of some mountebank doctor, some nostrum dispenser or other quack bent on bilking the populace, taking this spectacular and unseemly way of drawing attention. Those who could not read would speedily learn the meaning from others and hurry off to be duped.

No doubt of it—the English were a mad race.

But he glanced at John Kempton, who had doffed his cap and was making a low bow, graceful for a man of his bulk. Now he bellowed like Bow bells, "God save you, Queen Bess, Glory of England! God save Our Gracious Queen and give you long life!"

With a gesture of elation, he tossed his expensive cap in

the air, to its certain loss. "The Queen! The Queen! All praise to Our Sovereign Majesty!" he called above the crowd. In the surge of excitement, the clamor and clangor of the throng, he—whose eye and heart were ordinarily drawn to children—paid scant attention to a ragged girl at his side, saying in a tone of disappointment, "But she just about has no *teeth!*"

"The Queen! The Queen!" John Kempton boomed, quite beside himself with the joy of the moment.

Jan exchanged a glance with his brother, who shrugged slightly. Not only were the citizens of this country mad, but the Queen herself was in as bad case. Imagine the King of Spain *or* the Duke of Parma, who ruled Flanders for the Spanish Crown—just fancy one of *them* jostling about in the commonality as if he were *part* of it.

"Upon my word," he said in his brother's ear, "this lacks dignity!"

Nils, for all he was of two minds about Squire Kempton, would not have him offended. He glanced to be sure Jan's words had not been overheard, saw no need to worry.

For John Kempton, in a transport, had quite forgot the Flemings. "My cup, my cup," he whispered to himself, "truly it doth run over!"

Because, a moment past, the eye of Majesty had turned his way and rested on his features. He had received, here before the public gaze for all to see, a smile from the royal lips, a faint nod of the royal head.

His head spun; his knees grew weak; a tremor passed through his body; his vision blurred. It was the crowning moment of his life, never to be equaled. The Queen's Gracious Majesty of England, *Elizabeth Rex*, her very self, had met his eyes, had *smiled* upon him. Oh Lord! To see how he was favored, that had come from so mean a beginning! Here was a great marvel indeed!

She passed on, the crowd folding behind her like a wave running offshore, and John Kempton remained staring after, struck into a dream. He did not observe the departure of the Flemish merchants, who, growing impatient, moved on without him. They would not have crossed a room to secure a buss from the Duke of Parma or the King of Spain himself.

"She shows her years, this Queen of theirs," Jan said to his brother. "I doubt she was ever the beauty she was hailed."

"Plain as porridge, always has been. I saw her years since, in her heyday. It's the trimmings make that goose look glorious."

"An empire's ransom on her back," Jan said respectfully. He who, moments back, had held her adornments to be tawdry tinsel.

"Not that she's a goose in the *head*," Nils was quick to add. "As wily a ruler as the world has seen, this Queen of theirs. Mind how she kept all the princes of Europe dangling for decades in hopes of a match, when her only aim was to keep them from warring on England. She *plays* people like chessmen. Philip himself delayed his Armada for years, before seeing that his suit was hopeless."

"And then—what humiliation!"

"Ah, yes, this is a royal fox indeed. And one observes that her subjects still go mad at the sight of her."

"Perhaps, perhaps. To see their ruler, and in such fashion—*walking* like any commoner—cannot but astound and please the simple English populace. I concede, such bold behavior has made her the most successful monarch in Europe. Still, I think the mood of these Englishers is restless under so long a reign. They are warlike, and she has not permitted them much in that way. A few skirmishes in the peat bogs with Irish barbarians, some spats with Spain. Nothing to satisfy the eager appetites of young knights. 'England,' she has said, 'is wide enough for my ambition.' Ah yes. Peace has always been her care."

"Is peace not a good policy, Jan?"

"In a country squirming under too long a rule, swarming with an idle rabble, bored knights, a soldiery itching for battle and booty? I think not. Instead of honorably warring on foreigners, such as these begin to turn upon one another and anarchy results."

Nils, who did not much care how the English conducted themselves, so long as they continued to buy the fine weavings and lawn of Flanders, glanced backward. "Our ponderous friend is still struck into a statue."

"Well, well. Let us leave him. We'll meet tonight at the Clothworkers' dinner. That should give him time to regain his faculties. I still have a tooth for roast pig, brother. Let us press on. Notice how here and there, amongst the huzzahs, we begin to hear cries of 'Largess! Largess!'"

"Natural enough, Jan. The common herd always expects a shower of coins at the appearance of a monarch."

"Methinks, brother, that this shout for largess comes something hard on the heels of 'God save the Queen.' Ah! There is a fine stall." Jan quickened his steps toward an arbor where beneath the cool thatch were tables and benches. There a man could eat of roast pig, quaff brown ale, and generally find creature satisfaction.

Having jumped from the carriage, Will Shaw had sped into the crowd, grateful to be off, away from the enormous gentleman's booming voice and questions, vastly relieved to be out of that fancy gig with the nose-in-the-air coachman, the two high-stepping pretty horses with ribbons in their manes and tails. Would he ever see poor Casper again? Would Casper like a ribbon to his tail? Would he ever get some'at to eat again? Was he a runaway now, liable to the pillory or worse? Would Master Paston have the crier to cry his name through the streets, proclaiming him a truant 'prentice?

What was he thinking back there an hour ago—to go haring after those schoolboys when Master Paston had sent him for the trowel? What did Master Paston and Burt Crumb think had happened to him? Were they still waiting for the trowel? Did they care where he'd gone off to, maybe kidnapped, maybe pressed into naval service?

They'd be angry, very angry. How could he ever go back? How could he eat if he did not go back?

Had he stayed with that big, noisy, maybe crazy gentleman in the carriage, he'd have been given a morsel of food, surely. Of course, Will, he said to his listening ear, that was a fierce, loud man and awfully large, but I think meant no harm. He had seen through the scowling face to mild, kind eyes. Still, he didn't care for what he couldn't understand, and he surely could not understand why he'd been plucked from the roadside and pulled into the gentleman's coach in that fashion.

Now safely out of reach, he slowed his steps.

He no longer minded that he'd lost sight of the schoolboy lordlings and in a few moments had also put John Kempton out of mind, as his presence there was too peculiar to bear thinking on. Will knew what he wanted. He would walk till he found Kip-the-Pigman's stall, and there he would find Humphrey Mickle, and then—

And then?

If he did find the puppet man, what then?

Suppose Master Mickle misremembered him? Ah, no, no, no. Put that away, Will. He is a wonderful man who spoke you well and *said* where he was to be found. For what reason if not for you to find him? He will recall you. If you can find him.

Aimless, since with no idea of where the pigman's stall might be it made no difference what way he took, Will wandered, eyeing stalls where sweetmeats and custards glistened and shimmered, where trays of gingerbread boys were dark and crisply spicy, with raisin eyes and gilt buttons. He hastened on, faint from the cookie fragrance, only to encounter vast numbers of pies and tarts.

There were mountains of fruits. Pears and apricots and peaches and cherries he knew from seeing them in the Queen's orchards. Others—marvelous to behold—what were those? Foreign fruits, he guessed, and was right. There were artichokes, pomegranates, grapes, citrons, but Will could not name them. At a stand piled with golden globes, a woman cried, "Oranges! Luscious oranges from the hills of Spain! Buy oranges, good folk! Buy my oranges for your joy's sake!" Will had not seen any of these before. He lingered in front of each strange shape, like a viewer in a picture gallery studying still lifes.

Here were tables laden with bowls of nuts, baskets of hot bread. Trenchers of salted salmon, pots of kippers in oil. Eels a-frying! The odors dizzied. Though only a few feet from his hungry gaze, this rich fare might be spread atop a steeple for all he would get a nibble of it.

Folding his lips, swallowing hard, he stumbled past the stalls of foodstuffs to those that offered things to wear, things he, in his canvas smock, had no thought ever of owning and so did not covet, as he did the gingerbread boys. Nice to look at, Will, are they not? Gloves over there—embroidered with flowers and vines. Pretty things. Fans, all sizes, feathered, lacy, some of them silk maybe. Glitter of beads stuck on them. Here were purses, pomanders, powders. Saddles, shoon. Great lengths of cloth—some shining softly, some all embroidered with flowers, some of fine pale wool. The sort of cloth you saw worn around the palace of Whitehall, if you observed as you worked.

Will observed constantly.

Toys!

Little drums and fiddles, poppets and puppets (oh, where was Humphrey Mickle?). Willow whistles, reed slingshots, tops and balls and hobbyhorses! Toys, toys—for children who got to play with toys. There were none such on Seething Lane. But here was every kind of toy for a boy who had someone to give it him. He saw with his very eyes a man and a woman, holding a lad between them each by a hand, as if to protect him, stop at the toyman's stall and bend down and say—

They'd say to this boy that they would take home with them when the Fair was over, because he belonged to them, because he was their son and they wanted to keep him, "What will you have, Will? Choose what you will, Will!" That's what they'd say, or something like enough.

The boy put a thumb in his mouth while he looked

over the many choices. His parents waited, smiling. Will held his breath. *I'd* take the drum, he thought. Or the willow whistle. Or the—

The thumb popped out; a hand shot forward, folded over a bright wooden top. *There!* Not what Will would have chosen, but a nice top, a bright top, a top worth having . . .

Fetching a sigh for all that was here, and everything out of his reach, Will turned his gaze from side to side, shoved into confoundment by the clamor and clatter and color and confusion of this Bartholomew Fair.

Here were morris dancers!

Six men in motley jingled with tiny bells at waist and ankle. They leaped and kicked their legs out. They bounded and bowed. They moved 'round and 'round, circling, knocking their sticks together with a hollow, rhythmic clicking sound, tossing their sticks from one to another without one of them missing at all. Capering widdershins 'round the ring of dancers, wearing a hideous leering mask, wheepling like a mad thing, went a man on a red-maned hobbyhorse.

Will shivered and moved away. He watched a rope-dancer high overhead, skipping back and forth, just as if he were on the ground, turning somersaults with a basket of eggs in each hand. How could he do that and not drop a one?

On a sudden came a rush of cries from the distance, a thunderclap of salutation that shook the air.

"The Queen! The Queen! The Queen's Majesty of England!"

The shouts came on all sides, the whispers and glances and cries of doubt. Then yells of certainty. It was true, it was true! Great Elizabeth, her very self, was here, footing it through the Fairgrounds, touching her subjects, smiling upon them, permitting them to gaze upon her.

"Has any prince before this done the like?" said a man close to Will.

"She knows we weary of her and tries in this wise to woo us back."

"Traitor! Subversive! You should be stocked!"

"No, no!" cried the second man in alarm. "You misread me. I merely meant—she looks weary and—and wise—and—"

"I did not misread or mishear—"

"For God's sake! Don't repeat what I—*God save Her Gracious Majesty!* I am her loyal subject!" the second man shrieked, and fell to his knees.

Oh, the very sky was rent with the shouts of citizens hailing the presence of the Queen in their midst.

"When she leaves," Will heard a woman say, "she will scatter largess, surely. Let us hasten to try our luck!"

The crowd, including morris dancers, ropedancers, acrobats, hobbyhorse man, thundered off in the direction of the Royal progress, in hopes of a glimpse of Royalty, in greater hopes of scooping a coin at the finish of this open-air audience.

"Largess! Largess!"

Cries for alms mingled with blessings of God called down upon the monarch. Only the stallkeepers dared not leave their places, for fear of thievery. Glancing about, Will thought that most of them looked angry. Because they could not leave to view the Queen, to catch a coin perhaps? Or because her presence had drawn away customers?

Will, who had already seen the Queen, who was weak from hunger and almost without hope of finding Humphrey Mickle, sat on the ground and considered his own predicament, which was a lot harder than that of the vendors.

If he went back to the workshop on Seething Lane, he would spend the rest of his time of service—Master Paston claimed he owed five years yet—locked in the cellar at night, thrashed every day by Burt Crumb, and perhaps finally, in truth, clapped in the stocks and left there to the merciless mood of passing people.

But.

If he went back, he would get his loaf end smeared with lard twice a day and maybe a sup of cider. Maybe Mistress Cartwright would let fall another carrot from her window. The thought of food drew him, drew him. . . .

If he did not go back—what instead?

Getting to his feet, he bumped into a barefoot girl running past.

Merrycat had paused outside the wicket, knowing herself safe now from pursuit. Not that she supposed anyone would come after her. One washmaid more, one washmaid less—what difference in the vegetable kitchen?

Here was she, unnoticed and happy. She skipped along, nibbling a broad bean, eyes every which where, not much minding if she found the Fair or did not.

Like the children of the kitchen, like Will Shaw, like thousands upon many more thousands of London waifs, Merrycat had no notion, no interest even, in where or how she had been born, or to whom. She could remember no farther back than Agnes and the vegetable world she lived in, fairly content because she knew no else. This was the first that ever she had been away from that world, without an idea of where in this other world she now was.

Walking along the Strand, though she could not name it, she marveled at the crowds, the racket, the taverns and shops. What a lot of people there were in this town! Here was a blacksmith, leather-aproned, sweating in his hot forge, wielding a huge sledge above a glowing rod on his anvil. Next, a stoop-backed cobbler, his mouth bristling with nails, fashioning a boot. A pair of carpenters planed a coffin, right out on the street. Here an old woman sat in a booth, mending clothes.

And here was a plump, nice-looking lady making hats in a little shop. A sign above displayed an unwinding spool of thread, a feather, and a big needle. There were words, too. Merrycat, could she have read, would have learned that the milliner's name was Eliza Vestry. How pretty they were, the hats. Merrycat wondered what it would feel like, to have a thing like that on her head, all feathers and veils, like a crown. She wondered if the Queen wore her crown to bed. Would Agnes know?

More taverns, with gilt signs swinging above them. Merrycat liked the pictures. Flying pigs, coronets, lions on their hind feet. Her favorite was one with a swan with a head at each end of it.

People stumbled about, cursing, falling down, shouting at one another. They reeled down the streets, mumbling to themselves. Not just men. Women. Children. They leaned against the walls, lay in doorways, slouched along the ditches, heads down. Looking for food, Merrycat didn't doubt, thinking she'd not been grateful enough to have some'at to eat every day of her life. In the streets, in the path of traffic—heavy-wheeled carts, gentlemen's carriages, wheelbarrows—ran hollow-ribbed dogs, brown rats, and children in rags. Some hadn't even those, but ran in the day quite naked.

Everyone looked hungry. Merrycat decided she'd go back to Agnes. But not yet. After the Fair was over, she'd make her way back somehow and be where there was straw to sleep on, and always a bit of bread, and vegetable parings, and ale or cider to drink.

A red-faced woman came out of a tavern, shouting something cheery over her shoulder at those within. Merrycat dared to tug at her sleeve.

"Mistress?"

"Eh? Eh, what's this? What d'ye want, infant?"

"Where is this, please?"

Taken aback, perhaps at the "please," a word not often encountered, the woman looked down, not unkindly, and said again, "What d'ye want?"

"I want to know where is this?"

"Where is this, is it, you want to know? It is where you are, where else in the world would it be? Africky, mayhap?" She laughed at her own joke.

"But I don't *know* where is it?"

"Poh. It's London, right enough."

"Where in London?"

"Are you a noodle, sweetheart?"

"I don't think so."

"Most on us know where our feet stand at the moment. Are you lost, then?"

"No. Not in a way. I been thinking to find Bartholomew Fair and look at the sights. But where is it?"

"Ah. The Fair is what you seek. Well, now—do you see

all those shepherds and drovers herding their beasts up that street there?"

It would be a sight hard to miss—so many bawling, bellowing, bleating creatures, hurried along by hard-faced men in sheep's wool or leather cottes.

"So, look you, sweetheart. You and I stand this minute at Ludgate. Folly those herdsmen, you'll come to Newgate—the prison, you know. Pass through the Gate, out of the City wall, and you'll find yerself in Smithfield Markets, and there it is—what yer seeking . . . the fracas of the Fair."

"Are you going yerself, Mistress?" Merrycat asked, thinking it would be nice to be in the company of such a jolly, smelly, helpful woman.

"Sure not. Many's the time I've been, and what's to show? I fall straight into the pit of envy to see all the baubles and beads and stuffs of one sort or another that'll never decorate me fat self, for the thinness of me purse. No, no . . . get you along. I'll just step into this snug here."

She waddled off, with a backward wave, and Merrycat followed the herders toward Newgate.

Newgate Prison was very handsome, all turrets and towers and statues and carvings. She had heard that it was a terrible terrible place to be inside of, but from outside it was nice and fancy. She stopped to look at it for a moment, before walking through the great arch of the Gate.

And there! Here! She was outside the wall, in Smithfield at last! She, her own very self, was *at* Bartholomew Fair, and wouldn't Jack be jealous when she told *him*. If she saw him again. If she could find her way back to the palace and if Agnes didn't turn her out on the spot . . .

But no, no, no . . . Kind Agnes would not do that. And, oh, how much she would have to tell when she got back!

Stunned at the uproar and hullabaloo, at the vast stretches of stalls and tents and tables that seemed to go on for miles, bewildered by smells and shouts and colors that crisscrossed the whole air, she shifted from foot to foot, staring. Now the bells of London set up their hourly clamor, their ringing, tolling reminders of time and of God, so that the noise was greater than any she'd ever heard before, buried down there in the cellar with Agnes and Jack and the vegetables.

She stayed, tongue caught between her teeth, for a long time, but at length moved forward. If she didn't go in, she couldn't come out and so would have nothing to tell.

All at once her heart leaped at the fun of being herself, Merrycat, all by herself at the Fair! She rose to her toes, spun about, started running, bare feet flying over dust-thick lanes that ran between stalls, tangled, dirty hair flopping on her shoulders, a couple of broad beans still clutched in one grimy hand.

She ran right into a lad getting up from the ground, and for a moment they were *entwined*. Then Merrycat backed off, laughing. This was no one to be alarmed by. A lad about her own age, in a smeared canvas smock. At first he looked as if he were going to look angry; but then he smiled, and he had all his teeth. Teeth impressed Merrycat. Jack was missing a few, and Agnes had only three, dotted around her mouth. At present Merrycat had every one of hers. She supposed it wouldn't last; nobody ever seemed to keep a full set.

"The worst," she said now, "is the toothache. People go almost crazy with the toothache. I've never had one, have you?" The boy looked puzzled, so she explained. "Teeth! I was looking at your teeth and thinking how fine, but why do they always fall out? Wouldn't it be nice if they kept on growing? Like fingernails. That'd be good, wouldn't it?"

Will Shaw gave a shout of laughter. What strange people he was meeting today! First Humphrey Mickle, with his puppets and his long words. Then that huge man with the carriage. Now this grubby lass who talked about *teeth* and swung along beside him as if they knew each other.

About to start on one of the two remaining broad beans, she noticed how he gulped at the sight and held them toward him.

"Here. I've already eaten lots."

"Well," said Will, licking his lips, "I could take *one*."

"Poh. Poh, poh. Take both, I tell you. I don't want them anymore."

Closing his eyes, Will started to chew daintily, slowly, on a rubbery, dirt-smutted bean. A carrot, anyway half a carrot, this morning, and now two beans! Bliss.

They walked a bit, stopped, and stared at a dancer sliding easily on his rope overhead, holding a tumbler of water in each hand. He somersaulted! The two children held their breath until the ropedancer had safely curled his toes around his thin support, and not a drop spilled!

"How do you think he *does* that?" Merrycat said.

Will shrugged, wishing a ropedancer or an acrobat had found him in the alley and made a 'prentice of him. By now he would probably be able to do handstands and cartwheels.

"There was one back there, went head over heels with a basket of eggs in his hand. Didn't drop a one."

They walked on, deaf to the enticements of stall-keepers as those must be who have not a penny to spend.

"Look at *that*!" Merrycat exclaimed, pointing.

That was a glass beehive, tall as the man who stood beside it. He was explaining how by the use of this miraculous contrivance mankind could plumb the mystery of the bees' civilization.

"A society, good citizens, as orderly as any on God's wondrous creation. Further, I will demonstrate that I am able to extract the honey while in no wise disturbing the little beasties! They'll continue to work at their sweet task, knowing not me or my theft of their labor!"

"That's not nice of you!" Merrycat said loudly. "It's their honey!"

"Honey yourself," said the man, encompassing the crowd in his grin. "I leave them their share. We are partners, I and my bees."

"Do you believe him?" Merrycat whispered to Will, who said snappishly that he didn't know.

Then he added, "I suppose so. If he didn't share, the bees would starve, wouldn't they? Then what would be the use of his glass hive?" He stumped off, not caring if she followed. She did.

"You're hungry, aren't you?" she said.

"Yes." Will closed his eyes. He was terribly tired; his bones were sagging inside him. He wished he hadn't seen the schoolboys. He wished he'd gone for the trowel as bidden and brought it back to Master Paston. He wished he were back working on the wall.

He wished this girl would go away but, after a moment's silence, began to tell her about Humphrey Mickle and how he was hoping to find the puppet man, or Kip-the-

Pigman's stall, when he surely would find the puppet man nearby.

"I've been here for ages, going all around and going up and down, and I haven't seen a sight of either."

"Why don't you ask somebody where the pigman's stall is?"

"Ask? Who?"

"Anybody."

"How?"

"For dear's sake," she said, wrinkling her forehead, "you go up to a person and say, 'I want to know this; will you tell me, please?' Always *please*. Somebody long ago told me to say that, I forget who, but I always do and it's nice, people like it, like a nice old body I met back at—at Ludgate, it was, and she told me how to find the Fair, and she told better than Jack did, too—I was all mixed up with how he told me."

"Jack?"

"Never mind that. Let's get somebody to tell us where the pigman will be found." She flitted across to a stall-keeper almost buried behind beautifully tooled saddles and stirrups and silver fittings. In a moment she was back, saying, "He says we just keep going down that way"—pointing—"and pretty soon we'll find Kip-the-Pigman by the smell of his roasting pork."

Will ran his tongue over his lips. The two broad beans hadn't done much in the way of filling his stomach. He wondered if, even to see Humphrey Mickle again, he could withstand the smell of roasting pork without fainting. . . .

"Aren't you hungry?" he asked.

"I always am. Agnes doesn't stint us on vegetable

parings, and we get some'at of bread every day and a sup of ale, too; but just the same—"

"Agnes?"

"Back at the palace. I'm a washmaid in the vegetable kitchen. I was. I guess I am still. Will be. I'll go back, after we've seen the Fair."

Will liked that "we." He liked this girl. "What's your name?"

"Merrycat. What's yours?"

"Will Shaw."

"You have two. I've only one. Do you have a mother and father?"

"No."

"Neither do I. Agnes is nice enough. She's the head vegetable cook. Where do you live? Do you live someplace? Do you have a roof over you?" She was thinking of the children she'd seen wandering around Ludgate. They hadn't looked as if they had roofs to shelter under, feel safe under, the way she had.

Agnes was always telling them how lucky they were to have a roof above them. "London," Agnes would say, "for the matter of that, the whole country, for the matter of that, the whole *world*, is *crammed* and *burdened* with children like yerselfs tossed on the ocean of life and no one to toss them a plank, pluck them to safety, care about them the way I care about you lot. Count yer blessings, all of you, every day, and thank God on yer knees for the good fortune that brought you here to this kitchen."

Oh yes. She would make her way back to Agnes. . . .

She'd not heard the boy's answer about did he have a

roof or not and was about to ask again when the shouts of "Hail to the Queen" interrupted.

"Shall we go, shall we go?" she said, rising to her toes. "Shall we go to look at the Queen? She's down *that* way—" Pointing in the other direction from where the saddler had said the pigman would be found.

"I have already."

"Have what?"

"Seen the Queen."

"You *have*? How?"

"Working on the wall in her garden. Not close to, of course."

"Won't you come to see her, now, close to?"

"No."

"Well. Goodbye, Will Shaw!" She skimmed away, not looking back.

Will walked in the other direction and presently saw the pair of schoolboys idling along, eating pears and thick slices of bread. They seemed to be arguing. The one Will didn't like so well strode toward the tent where a Gypsy woman offered a peek at the future for a penny.

And now the other one, the nicer one, dropped behind him a piece of bread practically untouched! Will was on his knees with his hand on it before another hungry eye could spot the chance. Hardly dusty at all! Taking little bites, chewing slowly, eyes half-closed, he tasted for the first time bread such as this. So thick, and white, and crusty, and still warm. Fit for a king. Or a Westminster schoolboy.

Bliss.

"Let's hasten back to see the Queen," Jeremy said, elated at the opportunity.

"Why? She reminds me of school. I'm trying to forget it."

"But, Jones—" Jeremy began, and stopped. There was no way, he realized, to make Jones understand how he felt about the Queen. It was said that Her Majesty was aging; some said she might soon die—though that such a dire event could happen seemed past credence. How could she die and leave England all alone in the world? No—she would not do that. Still, she was old, and it seemed to Jeremy that nothing in the world was as important as the chance to look upon her whenever he could.

He wanted to rush back, to gaze upon her, to toss his hat in the air and shout *"God save the Queen!"* He could not. He dared not let Jones out of sight. Had Mr. Grant been here—if there was any imagining Mr. Grant at a Fair, which there was not—he'd have had them each by an ear, dragging them toward the Presence. This was surely the first time he'd ever wished for the Headmaster to be with him.

Angrily he submitted to what there was no avoiding: the necessity to keep a constant eye on Jones, whom he did not trust a farthing's worth. How, he asked himself for the dozenth time that day, was I ever such a fool as to get us into this? And will we ever be back in school, safely out of this stupid adventure that I have no one to blame for but myself?

Eating bread and pears, to which Jones treated, they moved along, Jones sauntering. He looks like a *fop*, Jeremy said to himself. Aware of ill temper rising in him like yeast in a loaf, he knew he'd have to keep it damped down. At bedtime, when darkness was falling in the dormitory and he was sore afraid, Jones might be spoken to sharply.

By day he was quick to take offense, quick to take whatever measure was at hand to even scores. Today he must not be crossed in any way, for fear he'd simply decamp. Now he paused to eye the acrobats, the ropedancers. Then stood for a while watching the morris dancers leap in a *click-clacking* ring, and the evil-looking hobbyhorse that capered 'round them counterclockwise.

"They make me shiver," he said, walking away. Jeremy followed.

They watched as a man extracted combs of honey from an enormous glass hive. A swarm of black and gold spangled bees justled about his head without stinging him.

"My father has seventy hives in his orchards," said Jones, studying the process with interest.

"Glass?"

"Of course not. This is but a novelty, Jeremy, designed to show the common folk what the inside of a hive looks like."

"The common folk? Should you be looking, then?"

Jones, more the little lordling as the morning passed, chose not to hear, or anyway not reply to, this impertinence.

Jeremy was tense, tired of the single company of his schoolmate, and increasingly apprehensive about getting back in the allotted time. Would Jones, now that he was away from school, even agree to *go* back? It was horribly possible that he would not, that somehow or other he'd figure a way to make tracks for his castle, his home, and his horse, Captain. That would leave Jeremy and Mr. Camden to sink together in the quicksand of Mr. Grant's wrath.

Jeremy had no idea how one could accomplish a journey from London to Sussex, with but a few farthings in one's pocket. Just the same, that cloud in Jones's head had a way of clearing when he found his interests seriously involved. Look how he ended up each morning with the whole blanket wrapped around him, leaving Jeremy tugging at it in vain.

"Jones," he said, "we can't stay much longer, if we are to get back as we promised Mr. Camden."

"Mmm."

"Jones! Did you hear me?"

"Look at that Gypsy woman, Jeremy! Listen—let's take a turn at her glass globe, see what the future holds for me. Come!"

It was plain what the future held for Jones. It held his father's domains, title, wealth. His father's stables. What did he need with a Gypsy to tell him that? Nevertheless, he walked over to the tent, stood with legs apart, hands on hips, like an imitation of King Harry, and said, "All right, Goody—for a farthing, let me in on what lies ahead. Just for the next few days, mind. Further than that, I already know. . . ."

God grant her crystal ball does not include travel instructions to Sussex, thought Jeremy.

Jones seated himself on the small stool opposite the seer, signaled to Jeremy with a careless hand. "You stay here behind me," he instructed. "Then you can have a turn, after."

"I don't want a turn. I want—"

But the Gypsy had Jones's hand in hers and his full attention.

The good bread was all at once dry in Jeremy's mouth, and he dropped it before entering the tent. He was shaking with fear and rage, angrier at himself than at this noble numbskull he slept beside every night. Who had dreamed up this folly? He had. Who had persuaded Mr. Camden that if they went, he and Jones, they would return promptly as bidden, the better for a short spell away from the schoolroom? *He* had, his own daft, dumb self. In a way Jones was not to blame at all. Being quite without ideas, he'd never have thought of going to the Fair. Once there he could only behave as he always behaved . . . selfishly, with no concern for anyone else.

Among their Latin readings, they had translations of the fables of that marvelous Greek, Aesop. Jeremy thought now of the cat turned into a maiden. She sat quietly at the board—until a mouse ran in front of her. Moral: The basic nature of man or beast does not change. Jones could not change his nature, and the thought of home and horses might be the mouse he'd run after today.

And the fault will be mine alone! Jeremy told himself bitterly.

He didn't need a Gypsy to predict what would happen if he was obliged to return to school without Jones. Resigned to being flogged this side of senselessness by the Headmaster, he was far more concerned about what would happen to Mr. Camden. Would they dismiss him for "derelict behavior"? How could I ever live with myself if they did that? Would they take away my scholarship? Would that matter to me if Mr. Camden is disgraced? What will ever matter again, after this day's work?

"Fool! Fool! Wretched, rash, unthinking fool!"

"Stop muttering," Jones said. "I'm trying to hear."

Please, God, Jeremy prayed silently, wishing he could get to his knees. Deliver me from this frightful *praesenti,* get the two of us back to school in time, and I'll never think up a scheme again in all my life. I will live by all the rules, I will do everything right and nothing wrong till the day I die, *semper* obedient—

Such a long-term promise, such a large undertaking, for the moment made his mind easier. *"Dum spiro, spero,"* he said to himself, or to the accompanying shade of Mr. Camden, who had bidden him speak Latin today. "While I breathe, I hope," he translated. In two languages it might be more effective.

"What are you nattering about?" Jones asked as they emerged from the Gypsy's tent. "I could hardly hear her for your mumble-mumble." Not awaiting an answer, he rushed on. "She is no fake fortune-teller, Jeremy. She knew *everything* about me, and of course, I've never seen her before, so how could she—"

"What did she know?" Jeremy asked glumly.

"That I go to school, am of high birth, that I will succeed to a title, that I love horses above all else in the world—"

"Jones! Do you suppose she found all that at the bottom of her smudgy glass ball? She *looked* at you, she *listened* to you! You're wearing a school uniform. You have the bearing of a tiny lordling. You wave your hand at minions the likes of me telling us where to stand. You drop a penny on her table as you would toss a sovereign to a beggar. . . ."

Jones said thoughtfully, "I don't think you a minion, Jeremy. You're my friend."

None so blind as those that would not see. Jones probably thought himself capable of friendship. It was possible that he did not know his air already was that of a knight of the lists, a peer of the realm, Master of the Horse to whoever happened to sit upon the throne when Jones was ready to succeed to the post.

"How did she know about the horses?" Jones said triumphantly. "Have you there, have I not?"

You probably told her yourself, Jeremy thought. Without realizing what you were doing, of course. Then she told you back what you'd told her. He judged it wiser not to disparage the Gypsy further. If Jones wanted to believe her, that was his affair.

"Did she tell you anything about your future? That's what I want to know." Did she tell you whether tonight you'll be in bed in the dormitory where you belong or posting through the dark toward home and horse while Mr. Camden and I bear your disgrace?

Jones frowned. "Now that you ask, no—she did not." He wheeled about, hesitated. "Should I go back and wring some word of the morrow out of her? She advertised a power to foresee, did she not? And foresaw *nothing*. Only told me what you have made quite clear she had no trouble deducing. Except the horses, of course. How would she—"

"Could we start back for school now? Please? It—our honor demands that—we gave our *word* that we would—"

"Of course," Jones said absentmindedly. "Hold! Here's a puppet show! And there's that urchin we saw on the King's Road this morning. I think he's following us. Maybe he's a spy."

As the ragged boy was already seated on the ground, gazing enrapt at the puppet drama, it seemed more likely that they were following him, but Jeremy was of no mind to start even a small difference with Jones. Don't in any way ruffle those feathers, and possibly we'll get back to school in time, and if ever I go crazy this way again, I will put myself over the flogging stool and *demand* my just punishment.

Punch was beating Judy over the head with a hammer, shouting, "Shrew! Cantankerous female crocodile! Hag of Hades! Pestilential petticoat tyrant! Take this!" He brought the hammer down as Judy swung about with a stout stick, catching him on the side of the head. "Brigand!" she screamed. "Bandit! Liar! Malicious maleficent malefactor!" She ducked down and disappeared as the dog came bouncing and yapping into the room, seized Punch by the seat of the pants, and began to worry at him, growling. Now Judy popped up again, the baby in her arms. The baby wailed; the dog yipped; Punch swore most horribly; Judy crooned to the baby, at the same time taking swings at Punch, this time with a huge ladle. In came the Doctor, demanding to know if anyone was hurt—

Jeremy was entranced. Considering how many citizens had rushed to the vicinity of Her Majesty, there was a pretty big audience for the little theater, and no wonder. This was a rare fine performance. He *loved* puppet shows and halted so firmly that Jones was obliged to stand with him.

"How many people do you suppose he has back there, to make such a racket in so many voices?" Jeremy wondered.

"Probably there's only the one. A traveling puppet man came by the castle once, and my father allowed him in to entertain at a party. He did everything his own self."

"Isn't that amazing? You wouldn't think one man could—"

But Jones was not listening, his attention caught by a pair of passing merchants. They spoke a tongue that sounded Dutch, was in any case foreign, but had just employed a word, common to all languages, that was sure to capture the ear of this horse-mad future earl.

Quintain.

"Listen, Jeremy! They speak of the quintain! You can hear from here the shouts of the riders! Let's to the field to see the sport!"

Jeremy looked at the sun slanting over the throngs of Fairgoers and Fair stalls. If he judged rightly, they had yet some time before being positively *obliged* to start back. If he tried to keep Jones from the quintain field, only rebellion would result. Whereas if he gave in—

"If we go and see a couple of gallops, can we start back right after that?" he asked, adding, when there was no reply, "You do see that if you fail to keep your promise, you will compass not just your own ruin but Mr. Camden's—and mine, and mine," he said softly. Would that weigh with Jones? He didn't know. He simply did not know.

Jones pushed his cap to the back of his head, stared around, at length met Jeremy's gaze. "Yours, I grant, and probably Mr. Camden's, but why mine? I should be in a mild disgrace, mayhap, for a short while. They might not permit me back at school, but what of that? I never wanted to be there. What use to me all those dead Romans with their—what does Mr. Camden call it?—their *furor loquendi*—means 'long-windedness,' doesn't it?"

"You know it does."

"Knowing what Cicero had to say about the Circus Maximus—if he had aught to say; did he?—never made a man sit a horse the better. As for reading, I don't think my father reads anything but lists from the stables and kennels. I'm not sure he can read anything else. *I've* never caught him out scanning his Horace. Half the nobles of England are illiterate, and not ashamed to be so. . . . Why should I know more than they?"

Jeremy took Jones by the shoulders, looked in the bland blue eyes. "Jones, will you promise that after you see a couple of tilts at the quintain, you will keep our promise to Mr. Camden? A true nobleman doesn't break his given word! Of all people, you, the future Earl of Tarleton, should know that. Maybe it will prove of little importance whether you know what Cicero ever said about anything, but it will be of vast moment that you are known as an honorable knight and earl. . . . Like your father—a man famous for integrity."

Probably the Earl of Tarleton had more foxhounds than principles, but one thing Jeremy knew: Besides being afraid of his father, Jones admired him extravagantly—the earl being a man noted for prowess in the Tilt Yard, endurance at the hunt. Speaking well of the father might be a way—perhaps the only way—to get this fool of a son to behave honorably. So—flatter him, curry him, pile praise on his sire. Kiss his foot! Anything to get him moving in the right direction.

"Of *that* I scarcely need reminding," Jones said now in his most forsoothly tone. One would not suppose a shade of betrayal had crossed his mind that day. "It is unbecoming in you, Jeremy, to suggest otherwise." Another princely wave of the hand, indicating that he took no offense.

Jeremy breathed a long sigh, and they proceeded to the sun-cracked field where in a far corner archers were shooting at butts, and, nearer to hand, riders at the quintain were hard at it.

"A simple diversion, for a passing good horseman," said Jones, now self-forgetful, an expert watching, with critical eye, an ancient sport at which he himself was already experienced and would, of course, by now excel were he not confined to school.

The quintain was merely a tall post, with a swiveling crosspiece on top, at one end a thick board, at the other a large sandbag. A rider came at the quintain full tilt with blunt-ended lance. He had to hit the board squarely, the trick being to get horse and himself out of range before the sandbag swung around and caught him on the back.

It was, for the first man, an easy feat. Trotting his mount to the far end of the field, he wheeled, came back at a gallop, lance extended, caught the board in the middle, and was well away before the sandbag was half around. The next rider was caught and unhorsed by the bag in a second. He lay sprawled on the browning grass, while the horse, that had taken no injury, put his head down and nudged him in a way that seemed to Jeremy almost consoling. After a bit the disgraced tilter got to his feet, led his horse back to the starting point, and remounted.

"Brave fellow," said Jones.

"He'll break his brave neck if he keeps on."

For this, Jones had only a glance of tolerant contempt. He turned his attention to another part of the field, where an ostler had horses at hire. Jeremy gave a start of dismay. "Jones! You are not—you are not thinking of—Jones, you are *not* planning a go at the quintain yourself?"

"Astride one of those poor nags? I'd as soon ride a ducking stool." But he shook his head sadly. A horse was a horse, and those pitiful beasts standing, heads down, subject to any fool rider with a farthing to spend, were of the species he adored.

"I'd like to *buy* the lot," he said. "I'd take them home and put them to pasture, let them do naught but graze and doze and dream until they die."

Jeremy glanced at his schoolmate curiously. This the lad who would kick a cat or dog out of the way as he would a pebble, who went forth with his slingshot after singing birds, whose greatest joy in life was to ride to hounds with his father, where anything from stags down to poor little hares was fair game.

It was plain, and they made no secret of it, or anyway, Jones did not, that the hunt was a substitute for what the Earl of Tarleton really wanted. War. Jones had whispered one night that his father was hoping Philip II of Spain would get another Armada together, one worth doing battle with, and come against England again.

"Suppose we lost next time?" Jeremy asked.

"With the Earl of Essex still alive to fight? That's treasonous talk."

"Your words are loyal to the Crown?"

"I am the *Crown's* liege servant. My father and I would have followed King Henry to the ends of the world. But this Queen avoids war as she would the plague. She lacks sinew. She didn't defeat the Armada. The Spanish defeated themselves. They builded their ships too high and heavy. And they had the bad luck of those terrible storms." His voice, his father's words. Either way, rash.

"A Queen who rides mounted to Tilbury to review her troops, with that huge Armada right offshore and yet a long way from defeated—she doesn't sound to me lacking in sinew," Jeremy had whispered furiously.

"You don't know what you're talking about."

"Neither do you. Will you please start your sniveling and get it over with, so maybe we can get some sleep? I'm *tired.*"

Only at bedtime could Jeremy speak in this manner to Jones, who not only was overcome nightly by his longing for home but was also afraid of the dark. By morning he seemed not to recall that the night before he had been impudently addressed by a carpenter's son. Jeremy had yet to decide if this was tact on the part of his bedmate or a sense of shame about the sobs he could not prevent, the fear of darkness he could not overcome. By daylight Jones would never admit fear of anything.

But he counts on me, Jeremy thought now, to keep his night terrors and his seditious talk to myself. He counts on me to protect him from the fists of those fellows at school—and there are plenty—who can't stand either his bragging or his bawling. Of course, Jones also had his followers and flatterers, the fawning instinct of the Court being caught early in life.

Once Jeremy had asked Mr. Camden please to let him share a bed with someone other than Jones.

"Your reason?" the Undermaster had inquired.

"Well, Sir—he cries every night. I don't get much sleep."

"The entire dormitory hears that."

"But I'm right beside him! He shakes the bed. Most of the others get to sleep long before I do." About to add that Jones took the whole blanket to himself every night, he refrained. That would sound *petulant.* Mr. Camden, every now and then, would say to a complaining boy, "Rage is permissible. Peevishness is NOT."

So far as Jeremy could see, rage, too, would have to wait until one had put school behind one and assumed the mask and mantle of the grown world. Already he had little confidence in that world.

So—Jones counted on him in many ways. In what manner could he count on Jones? He turned to put the question, and ice seemed to form on his bones.

Jones was not to be seen. Jones was gone.

Back at the puppet theater, things had taken a dramatic turn. Judy had caught Pretty Polly and Punch in an embrace!

"Philanderer! Base, villainous jackanapes!" she screamed, seizing the ladle. She clouted her husband on the head, then turned to Polly. "Hussy! Falacious, flirtatious flibberty-gibbet! Fie on you—I'll funnel you into a midden! Take that! Take that and that!" She swung 'round and 'round with the ladle, and Polly flopped out of sight. Judy grabbed the baby out of its cradle and threatened to throw it out the window.

"No, no!" said the Doctor, rushing in on the back of Dagonet, the horse. "Don't do that! It will damage the baby badly to be dashed to the ground in this wise! Here, let me take it," he said, dismounting. Judy tossed the bundled baby at him. Exit Doctor and baby in one direction, horse in another. Enter the Constable.

"All here under arrest! By order of Justice Highfever! All follow me to the Pye Powder Court, now in session, Justice Highfever presiding!"

Punch threw the ladle at the Constable, who screamed

and fell out of sight. Then he began to thrash the dog, who yipped wildly, bringing Jack Catch on the run, swinging a hangman's rope.

"Somebody here screamed for me?" said Jack Catch. "I heard a yelp of pain. Is hanging called for?"

"You heard the dog," Punch growled. "Get you gone, or I'll give you some of what I've been giving him."

"No, no, no. I care not for beating. Just tell me, is there anyone here for the long drop today?"

"I'll long drop you!" yelled Punch, kicking the dog and starting after Jack Catch, who ran offstage.

All at once several children in the audience began to shriek.

"Punch! Punch!" they warned. "The Devil is coming! The Devil is right behind you!"

In he came! Bounding up and down, twisting and twirling, red rags fluttering about him like flames, he waved his forked tail, turned his horned head from side to side. Oh, what an evil grin was fixed on his rufous face.

"Punch!" screamed the children. "Oh, Punch, you're in trouble now!"

Too late! The Devil made off with Punch, and one by one the others popped up and hurtled offstage after them . . . Jack Catch, the Constable, the Doctor riding Dagonet and clutching the baby, the dog yapping, Pretty Polly crying, and finally Judy, who grabbed up the ladle and flew past, waving it aloft and calling out, "I'll to the rescue, Punch . . . never fear!"

The curtain came down; the audience applauded; Mr. Mickle came out from his box and smilingly handed his hat around. It did not seem to Will Shaw, gazing at the puppet man with admiration, awe, and the seed of love, that much was put in the hat, but Humphrey Mickle seemed not to care. He announced that another show would be forthcoming in an hour, and gradually the spectators dispersed.

Among these was John Kempton, lagging so far behind the Flemings as to lose touch with them. He had paid some heed to the puppet show, a rare good one, but mostly his attention had been on the ragged boy he'd been looking out for all morning. Clearly the lad was wrapped, as in a blanket, with infatuation for the puppeteer. The child hung back, making no attempt to approach the showman, but equally making no move to leave the vicinity.

Frowning, John Kempton made for the puppet master.

"Sir," he trumpeted, "may I congratulate you on a dramatic triumph?"

"Well, now," said Humphrey Mickle, taken aback by Mr. Kempton's scowl but pleased with his words, "I take that kindly. My poor little show scarcely merits—"

"I'll have a word with you, if convenient?" John Kempton boomed.

Whyever not?" the puppet man said mildly. "However, I was planning a short recess over there at Kip-the-Pigman's stall. Dramatic triumphs make a man hungry. And thirsty."

"I'll accompany you. Allow me to treat you to—"

"No need, no need of that."

"It would be my pleasure," Squire Kempton said loudly.

"Well. Well, then—if you insist."

"I do."

It crossed Mr. Kempton's mind that possibly he insisted too much? That he might offend? Oh, dear, oh, dear—how difficult to overcome habit. However, too late to rescind his offer, and it was obvious that the puppeteer was not garnering a great sum for his efforts. Perhaps would be glad of a free meal? On the other hand, perhaps would take offense.

Well, well, let it stand. . . .

Perspiring a little, as he always did when, after the fact, he felt he'd behaved foolishly, but resigned to his own shortcomings, John Kempton followed the puppet master across to Kip's stall, where people at tables under the thatch were eating their fill of excellent roast pork, drinking their fill of mulled ale, and sat themselves down.

"John Kempton, cloth merchant, Sir, at your service," said Mr. Kempton, after he had ordered two of the best from the tapster.

"Humphrey Mickle, at yours, Squire," said the puppet man with an air of bewildered but good-humored interest.

"Don't turn your head just yet, but across there, close to your theater—by the way, are you keeping an eye on your possessions? You seem a pretty careless fellow—" Feel him out, get a latch on his character! Mr. Kempton had a plan but needed to know something of the man opposite before committing himself. He did not, especially, mind being thought foolish himself, but had no mind to play ducks and drakes with the life of a lad he intended to help.

"No," said Humphrey Mickle. "That is, yes, I am watching the booth. Notice that I seated myself so as to face it. I'm quick on my feet and would be a match for anyone who wanted to make off with—" He, too, interrupted himself. "I thank you, Squire, for this excellent repast, but I must needs wonder, do we near the point of your matter?"

John Kempton quaffed a few mouthfuls of ale, pushed his lips in and out, scratched his chin, leaned across the table, and said, "That lad, do you see him without being obvious—over there, lingering near your box?"

Humphrey Mickle glanced across the road, and exclaimed, "By His Lids! That's Will Shaw!"

"You know him?" said Mr. Kempton, somewhat put out.

"Not that. Not know him. I encountered him early this morning in Seething Lane. He's the captive of a surly brute of a journeyman mason, and it's my belief that the mason himself, one Peter Paston, has persuaded the lad to think he's articled as an apprentice. It's my further belief that he's no such thing. I doubt there are any papers. Probably the boy was just taken from a gutter and told a pack of lies. What is your interest in him?"

"Mr. Mickle, let me confide. From the meanest beginnings I am come to be a rich man but am without family. No kith, no kin. I give, generously I make bold to say, to the poor. I help where I can—where I can—trying to share my good fortune."

"Allow me to congratulate you, Sir. It has been my observation that wealth more often engenders selfishness and greed than openhandedness. Yes, yes . . . this is admirable. But, again, are we somewhat near the matter of your concern, either with me or with that urchin? Look there— he seems to be guarding my box as if I'd charged him to—"

"He is taken with you, Mr. Mickle. I could see that plainly as your show progressed."

"We had a pleasant few minutes together. Further, I had occasion to put the journeyman out of countenance. No doubt Will enjoyed that. He's a good enough young fellow, and not, that I could descry in our brief exchange this morning, either sullen or—or bitter. From what I saw of that nasty piece of goods, the journeyman, he'd have a right to be both. But how come you have aught to do with him?"

"This morning, as I drove toward Smithfield in my carriage—that is, I wish to be precise—not *my* carriage, but one I hire for the nonce, until—but that's by the way—I saw him sitting on the roadside, tired and footsore. I offered him a ride."

"That must have startled him! Did he accept?"

"I talked him into it."

More likely scared him into it, thought Humphrey Mickle. Here, it was plain, was a kind and generous and probably lonely man who charged like a bull at an object of benevolence. The amalgamation of a massive presence, an obviously unintentional frown, and a voice like the lion's roar no doubt subdued what reluctance he encountered.

"I expect Will had a happy time, riding in a carriage?" Humphrey Mickle ventured.

"Behaved as if I were abducting him."

Ah. As I thought, said Mr. Mickle to himself. That Will Shaw was a stiff-spined lad, he'd already gathered. It was not surprising to find him ungrateful and uncomfortable with a rich merchant's charity pressed upon him, no matter how footsore or hungry—

He let out an exclamation. "Here we sit talking, and

that poor boy probably feels his stomach pushing against his backbone from hunger! Let us call him over!"

"No, no," said Mr. Kempton, for once restrained. "He would take that in the same fashion as he took my ride—"

"I don't think so. He's used to walking. Used, no doubt to hunger, too, of course—"

"Let me come to the point, Mr. Mickle."

"Please do, Squire Kempton."

John Kempton leaned across the table and began to speak earnestly of what he had in mind, while Will Shaw, huddled near the puppet man's booth, watched wonderful Humphrey Mickle eat of roast pig and drink of ale with that altogether peculiar gentleman of the fancy carriage and the cross coachman.

Once they glanced his way, and he nearly decided to move on. But by now too weary and hungry to make a decision, he remained. Maybe, after a while, he could creep over behind Kip-the-Pigman's booth and find some scraps dropped on the ground, the way that piece of bread had been thrown down.

Had he been by himself, back in the cellar of the workshop, he would have put his head down and cried tears, as he did often enough when he was alone. But he was either too cowardly or too shy to risk tears in public. He did wrap his arms around his knees and rest his head on them and wish things it was too late to wish about. . . . That he had gone for the trowel. That he had not seen the schoolboys. That he had not followed them.

He wished he had never heard of Bartholomew Fair.

AFTER THE FAIR
WAS OVER

idnight.

From all the steeples of all the churches of London, bells told the close of day, and would now be silent until five o'clock and dawn. Shortly after, the watchmen of London moved along the dark streets within the walls, carrying their lanterns, calling the hour. "Past twelve o' the clock, on a thick, misty morning! All is well!"

The carillon of St. Margaret's was nearest the palace, and Bettice Coyne counted each stroke as she peeled the trappings of majesty from England's Queen. First the high-standing ruff with its bugle beads and pearls embedded in stiff lace, the jeweled chains, which seemed to have grown weightier since morning, the rings, bracelets, aglets, and gold fringe. The gold and enamel emblem of St. George. With all that laid aside, she had removed the velvet robes, the silken undergowns, the farthingale hoop, the chemise, the hose, the brilliantly buckled shoon, to come at length upon the woman who stood beneath this harvest of adornment.

Small, wrinkled, shivering until the warm wool nightrobe was dropped over her head, the nightcap placed on wispy gray—erstwhile golden-red—hair, the Queen of England, shorn of all that marked her apart from other souls, knelt beside her great bed and clasped her hands in silent prayer, while Bettice stood aside, waiting.

What does she pray for? wondered the lady-in-waiting. Long life? She's had that. A little while to go yet, but most behind her. Power? No need to ask Heaven for what had been so fully granted. Health? Too late for that. She will not give in. Carries herself as straight as ever, drives herself and all at Court as hard as ever, works as long hours, dances till all hours, goes to the Fair a-foot, rides to the hunt, shouts and loses her temper and laughs and—does not give in.

Still. She is failing. All the Court sees that, and watches. Waits.

As Elizabeth dropped her head upon her hands, Bettice found a seed of grief within herself . . . for that the Queen was growing old, for that old age had hunted her down. For that the world would be an unknown sea when this Queen died.

When she died?

Could Elizabeth die? Now Bettice shivered. She herself,

most of England, had known no other monarch. Wanted no other.

Was this true? Had there been, in the crowds today, a tinge of boredom in the shouts of greeting, the tossed caps, the cries of blessing upon Her Majesty? More shouts of "largess" than in progresses hitherto?

Elizabeth stood, turned, smiled, and all at once Bettice understood that this woman did not require trappings to be what she was . . . the Queen of England, the greatest prince the land had ever known.

"We have had a long day, have we not?" said the Queen to her lady-in-waiting.

"Yes, Your Grace. But a fine day."

"Perhaps. Yes, I will grant, on the whole, a fine day. Yet I think—" She sighed, smiled again. "No matter what I think. Do you know, Bettice, that I was young once? Long ago, of course. Long, long ago."

"Oh, Madam—"

"And then—in that long ago—the world was divided for me, as for you now, with old people and young. *I*, of course, was young, and so would always be. This is what you, and that minx Jane, and the rest of the Court believe: that youth is your province, and you will dwell there forever. Dear God, *how young you all are*! Hardly a one of you near my age. Only Burghley, only Burghley is left me . . . to love, to share remembrance with. Oh, kind remembrance!"

She lifted her beautiful hands, let them fall. "Well, too much of that. I believe I am weary enough to sleep. Perhaps tonight soundly, and then I'll not keep you awake. Let us hope so."

Bettice dropped to her knees. "Dear Madam, I wish you a good night's rest, but if you wake me, I am happy in that, too. I am yours, in all love and obedience."

For a moment the blue eyes of Royalty misted. Only for a moment; but Bettice saw, and the seed of grief flowered into pain, for the Queen's sadness and for her own mortality. She had never thought, until this night, until this moment, that not queens alone grew aged and knew sorrow and discerned the profile of death. Her Majesty was right. As she was always. I, thought Bettice, and that vixenish Jane, and the rest of us here in Court, fluttering mothily around this once glorious, now flickering candle, think that to be young is our *right*, that youth is our *part* of life. We think that only *old* people are old.

Time, she said to herself, only half-believing, will surprise us, too. I wonder how brave we shall be.

As the lady-in-waiting turned away, there came again the high, thin voice, muffled behind velvet draperies. She drew them back, leaned in a little, and whispered, "Did you call, Your Majesty?"

"No, Bettice," came the answer. "Snuff the candles and go to bed."

"Made it back to us poor folk, did yer?" said Jack when Merrycat drooped into the kitchen late in the evening.

"I'm here, amn't I?"

"Did you ever make it to *there*, is what I wonder. Did you set foot in the Fair at all, I ask meself."

"I did."

"That's all well, but I say, Who's to say you didn't if you say you did?"

"Why would I say I did if I didn't?"

"Show off to the rest of us, mayhap? Us that stayed to home and did our jobs and didn't get to mingle with nobs at the Fairgrounds . . ."

"Whyever would I show off to the likes of you?"

"Oh, aye . . . above yerself, is it now, just because you had enough brains in yer head to find the Fair and get back again— The likes of *us* is the likes of *you*, let me point out before we get further along in life. . . ."

"Hush up!" Agnes snapped. "You both stop yer nattering. Now, Merrycat, tell us everything you saw and said and did and thought and ate since you ran away this morning."

"I didn't eat," Merrycat said hoarsely. "Except a handful of broad beans from the garden and gave two of those to a boy looked hungrier even than me—"

Agnes, honoring the adventurer, put a piece of bread in front of her . . . and then a mug of milk! This was a drink none of the other children had tasted. It was the Queen's milk, for the making of soups, also a creamy mush of vegetables that Her Majesty relished. Merrycat sipped cautiously at first, then with ecstasy, slowly running her tongue across her lips to catch out any missed drop.

"Poh, poh," Jack muttered. "If *that* is to be the runaway's reward, I'll be off meself in the morning. . . ."

No one paid him heed as the kitchen children crowded 'round Merrycat expectantly, jealous of the milk but even more anxious to hear of the world beyond this vegetable kitchen. Agnes leaned her thick arms on the table and said again, "Tell, tell . . . who knows which of us here'll ever see the great Fair? Start with the beginning, how you got there. . . ."

"I gave her directions!" Jack said. "I know me way

about London, I do—born in Cheapside I was, and lived out there in the streets until the misfortunate day that—"

"Jack!" yelled several of the children. "Leave off! We want to hear Merrycat!"

She, dreamily sipping milk, told what she could remember, made nothing up, nodded toward sleep, revived, talked on, was about to subside into silence when she remembered: "Oh! I looked at the Queen!"

"Did you do that, now!" Agnes was impressed. "And how was Her Majesty looking this day?"

"Fancy."

Agnes glared. "That's all you have to say to us who've never clapped eyes on the Lady at all though we slave for her down here every day of our lives? *Fancy!* You can tell us some'at more than that, Miss Truant, or I'll sconce you tomorrow's supper."

Merrycat thought a moment. Then: "She just about doesn't have any teeth."

Agnes, who had but three of these herself, stood abruptly and flapped her apron at them. "All right, the lot of you—off to sleep. Don't think I'll let you lie about in the morning. You—Merrycat! If ever you run off this way again, you'll not be getting back in. I'm clear?"

"Yes, Mistress. Thank you, Mistress."

On her bed of straw, Merrycat drew her smock over her knees. Maybe she should not have said that to Agnes, about the teeth. It was not all she remembered of the Queen. Or even most. Mostly she could see again how Her Majesty had turned and smiled upon the big gentleman who was shouting her name, and calling blessings down upon her, and crying tears.

It seemed funny, to the washmaid, that a grown-up

man should cry in that fashion just because an old lady smiled at him. Even if the old lady was a Majesty.

Drowsily she said to herself, *That's* why the Queen likes mush of vegetables so much. Because she doesn't have any—anyway hardly any—*teeth.* . . . A Queen could do just about anything she wanted—wear all those shiny clothes with jewels hung all about her so she rattled as she walked, eat all she wanted even if she didn't seem to *want* much—and couldn't keep her teeth any more than Agnes. . . .

As the bells of St. Margaret's tolled midnight, Merrycat fell asleep, thinking how wonderful milk tasted, wondering if she'd ever taste it again. For her, the mug of milk was the best part of this day of Bartholomew Fair.

At the far end of the dormitory, just outside the small room where Mr. Camden slept, a horn lantern burned all night. Its light was dim, almost too shuttered to be seen, but it was there. By that forlorn glow a pupil could, in absolute necessity, get up in the night. A need of nature, a sudden illness—these were about the only reasons found acceptable for stirring from bed before morning.

Loneliness was faced in silence. Terror of the dark, which more boys than Jones suffered from, was endured. Fear of being unable, the following day, to gloss lines of Quintilian for Mr. Grant, was beaten down as best a boy could manage. There was no choice; the morrow would see him either successful or flogged.

They faced the fear of dying, too.

One morning at dawn, two years before, when the bell ringer arrived to rouse the room, one Queen's Scholar had failed to heed the summons. In the night, in the middle of the dark, without a sound of protest that anyone heard, he had died.

"That's what he did," the pupils whispered to one another, shivering. "He *died.*"

There were those who still lay awake for hours, dreading a sleep from which they might not waken. They didn't bawl or whimper, keeping others from sleep, as Jones did with his longing for home and horses. They quietly stared into dark space in an effort—always defeated—not to lose consciousness.

"Do you ever get afraid that you will die?" Jeremy had asked of Jones.

"Of course not! I'm too rich to die."

Jeremy had not put the question again. And for the most part, he fell asleep without fear of death or the dark or Latin, as quickly as Jones's nightly lamentations permitted.

Tonight, lying with his back to his bedmate, looking toward the dim and distant lantern light, he felt a simmering fury that was going to cost him this whole night's sleep. He knew it, and could do nothing to suppress his rage, which in this case was surely permissible.

Jones, for once, wasn't crying. He was whispering urgently about how he should be forgiven forthwith because after all, he *had* come back, hadn't he? He hadn't really run off to his father's moated and crenellated and infinitely battlemented castle in Sussex. He'd *started* to, then had honorably done what any honorable fellow would do, and how Jeremy could keep on being angry this way was more than he could understand, was in truth more than he was prepared to tolerate and if Jeremy kept on this way—

"Stop!" Jeremy said. "Just do not . . . ever . . . talk to me again about anything at all. Don't say good morning to me, don't say good night. And don't—just *don't*—ever after this ask me to help you with any part of your lessons again. You do the best you can on *your own*, for the rest of the time we're in school."

He felt Jones go rigid with anger and was pleased.

"I do not propose to let a—a—" Jones began, then held back "carpenter's son," though the slur quivered in the air between them. Where his concerns were involved, Jones was a prudent person, and there was no getting around it; without Jeremy he had little chance of retaining a fingerhold on cursed Cicero, or awful Ovid, or horrible Horace. Mr. Grant had been known to expel even a duke's son who simply could not learn. Perhaps the duke in question had been more lenient than the Earl of Tarleton would be in a similar case. The thought of his father's reaction, should he fail out of Westminster, was daunting—most daunting.

No, better to humble himself before this upstart carpenter's sprout than be tossed out of school *or* take more floggings than necessary. He'd get enough of those in any case, because he kept forgetting what Jeremy instructed him in.

Why did his father keep him in this wretched, useless, mind-bungling, spirit-destroying prison? Would he ride the better for knowing what Caesar had to say of horses? Become a finer tilter for understanding how Marcus Valerius Martialis viewed the Circus Maximus? Would he, if ever England regained her natural right to war on other nations, be less the soldier, less the fighter, if he'd not learned a line of Latin at all?

It was Jones's settled theory that his father kept him at Westminster in order to keep him out of the way—jealous of a son already tall as himself, and counted the superior horseman. Couldn't write his own name, but would wall up his heir for years on the pretext that an earl's son must have a classical education. And why? Because this peace-mad Queen was overeducated herself. Was there no way to rise at Court without jabbering in a moldy tongue?

Jeremy said the Earl of Essex knew five tongues well and a few others to nod at. If the Earl of Essex felt it becoming to play at languages, mayhap he himself should try. . . . He sighed and addressed himself to the problem at hand . . . this mulish schoolboy here in the bed beside him, without whose help he'd surely founder.

To be fair—Jones prided himself on being, on the whole, fair to others, even inferiors—Jeremy had been unlikely clever to get them the day's opportunity. And Mr. Camden had been monstrously indulgent to give it them. In truth, he didn't *want* Jeremy to lose his chance of advancement in the world, which he'd not get without schooling. Nor did he want Mr. Camden, who was a good man, and a kind, to lose his position, be cast out disgraced, as he surely would have been if Mr. Grant had found him out in this day's escapade.

But damme, he said to himself, I *did* come back, we *are* here, and no one the wiser. So why is Jeremy still in a temper with me?

Gritting his teeth, he mulled over ways of dissolving Jeremy's astounding, never-before-encountered irritation. Well, something stronger than that. The fellow was actually in a wrath . . . actually beside himself. For the matter of that, completely *above* himself, going on this way when nothing had happened except probably he'd had a slight scare. . . .

Standing there at the quintain, watching the riders, none of whom could have stood against himself, for all they were older and so had ridden more years and more nags, nodding as this rider dodged the sandbag, laughing heartily to see that one toppled, he had all at once, resistlessly, been stricken with a longing for home, for the unmatchable sensation of riding to hounds on that glorious hunter Captain. He hadn't seen Captain in *months*. Almost without thinking, he had walked away from Jeremy and, before he knew it, was lost in the crowd, still puzzling a way to get himself home. By the time he'd come to his senses, recollecting how rash was even the *idea* of arriving unbidden at the castle, he couldn't find his fellow Fairgoer.

Not for a while. Then, to his amusement, he'd spied Jeremy rushing in one direction, turning to dash in another, face a mask of terror, sweat staining his clothes, eyes starting out of his head as if to leave it entirely. Awfully funny, even if Jeremy couldn't see it that way. When he'd walked up and clapped him on the back, saying, "What ails thee, nervous wight—art lost?" Jeremy had turned upon him a look that made him both furious and ashamed. A look that reminded him of something he could not immediately recall. Then, shuffling in memory, he recollected a glance of contempt with which his father had dismissed from his presence a knight discovered in a lie, a man fallen short of knightly standards.

Beyond ascribing it to envy, Jones didn't trouble himself about why he was unpopular at school, but from no one before had he encountered such an expression of scorn. Despite the difference in their stations, for a shriveling moment he felt inferior, as if *he*, the future Earl of Tarleton, had fallen short of *Jeremy Hensbowe's* standards. This was an insupportable sensation, and the only refuge he could find was jauntiness.

"What's wrong with you?" he asked, attempting a laugh. "You should see yourself, Jeremy—running around like a rooster without a tail. It's not *my* fault if you got lost."

In flat, cold tones, Jeremy said, "The only reason you didn't go through with it is that you're afraid to face your father."

"Go through with what? I don't underst—"

Then, of all maddening, shaming things, he'd had to run after Jeremy for the second time that day. The fellow's pride was appalling.

"You wrong me!" he'd said. "I confess I *did* think of trying to go home—I mean, can't you understand how I get this terrible *need* to see Capt—I mean, my mother—"

"What I understand is that you'd have left me and Mr. Camden in the quicksand without a thought for how we'd get out. *If* we could get out. What I understand, too, is I don't want to look at you or listen to you anymore. Ever."

He'd walked rapidly away, with Jones tagging after, all the way back to school.

Now here they were—enemies in the dark. Surprising himself, Jones gave a moan of pain at the thought of Jeremy's lost friendship.

"Jeremy, please—" he began, then broke off in astonishment.

Jeremy had rolled off the bed and under it!

For a moment Jones was too startled to react at all.

Then he leaned over, groping with his arm, trying to make contact somehow. He had a frenzied feeling that he must touch Jeremy, must retrieve his friendship somehow, or everything would come apart for him. "This is crazy!" he whispered. "You'll get the ague down there. Come back up here, Jeremy, you fool!"

Under the bed, on the cold stone floor, already violently shivering, Jeremy knew he would not have self-management enough to spend the night here. It would have given him much satisfaction to lie here till dawn—maybe getting the ague—but he was neither stupid nor heroic enough to bring it off.

Manifestly Jones was desperate to reconcile, not alone for the sake of help with his lessons. He had no other friend, and Jeremy was, or had been, for the most part, his friend—did, for the most part, in spite of his ridiculous airs, like him. Because we're used to each other? Jeremy wondered, trying to wait as long as possible in this icy, coffinlike space, before being forced to climb back up to the bed. Because I know he depends on me? A shabby reason for friendship, probably, but with Jones it was not easy to find grand ones.

All at once Jones began to giggle. "Jeremy! This is daft, this is moony! Come back up here and I'll—I'll let you have the blanket all night! Anyway, you can have your half. All night. That's a fair offer now, isn't it?"

Jeremy crept stiffly up and got under the blanket, grateful for its warmth, for the warmth that Jones had created simply by lying there. He supposed it was wrong to be critical of a person like Jones, who had blood too blue and skin too thick for ordinary understanding. Either take him as he was, or get Mr. Camden to assign him another bed.

Since he'd already tried that and failed, the next best course was to accept Jones with his many impregnable faults and his few puny virtues.

"Are we friends again?" Jones whispered.

"Yes. Go to sleep."

Before the bells of St. Margaret's had done striking twelve deep midnight notes, they were asleep, the one too tired to be angry, the other too tired to cry, both glad that their day at Bartholomew Fair had come to an end.

In a corner of the field where the archers and quintain riders had had their sport, the tents and caravans of the entertainers were now grouped. Tomorrow they'd disperse, to travel the roads, visit towns and hamlets, inn courtyards and castle halls, displaying their several arts and acrobatics, making a living in this wise, as other folk made theirs in settled labor.

Some had gone to sleep, but many were awake still, counting the day's take, visiting back and forth, speaking of successes—or failures—in capturing the crowd's attention and applause. A few were roistering, to the annoyance of the many.

Will Shaw, mistrustful of his situation, certain he was either dreaming or the victim of a mistake, sat hunched and unspeaking on the floor of Mr. Mickle's little caravan, trying to sort out his day. From the moment he'd run after the schoolboys till this minute, everything seemed unreal to him.

He was *not* in the cellar, dreaming—he knew that. But had it all taken place—that ride he didn't want in the noisy gentleman's carriage, that little girl who gave him two broad beans and then ran after the Queen, and finally the puppet man that he'd met up with in Seething Lane this morning—he was *here with that same man*?

It was all true?

He had eaten more today, he thought, than in all his life before put together, fed not just by Mr. Mickle but by that enormous loud man who looked so angry but acted kind, who'd given him the ride that morning. The two of them had called him into Kip-the-Pigman's stall and told him to eat his fill. As he had done, gobbling, scarcely remembering to say thank you, for fear they'd decide it was some other boy they'd meant to feed and not himself at all . . . he'd get it all down before they changed their minds.

Now here he was, his own self, in this snug little place that Mr. Mickle called his caravan. It had an oil lamp that had a nice odor and made the little room look soft and rosy. Will had not seen a lamp before, and very few tallow candles. In the workshop of Peter Paston, when it got dark, you lay down on your straw and stayed there till morning. Mr. Mickle had a cot with blankets on it. A piece of material on the floor. Rug, Mr. Mickle called that. Outside, it was foggy and growing chill, but he, Will, was in here, warm and *not hungry*.

How long would this last? When did he get sent back to Master Paston? To Burt Crumb. To the straw and the cellar and the stale bread and lard, and the bricks, the bricks, the bricks.

"Cat got your tongue, lad?" said the puppet man. Will continued silent, unmoving. "You will find, Will, that I am a man given to verbosity. Not, I pride myself, a prattler, but admittedly a loquacious party. Therefore, a measure of communication between us will be necessary if we

are to remain together, living, as it were, con-
terminously. . . ."

All of this that Will caught were the words "remain
together." Us? he thought. Him and me? *Remain* together?
How did he mean? For the night? Then back to Seething
Lane and Burt Crumb and the cellar? For longer? Stunned,
unable to form a sound, he stared into the man's face, trying to read it.

Humphrey Mickle pursed his lips, stared about,
reached into his sack, and brought out Pretty Polly.

"Will Shaw, Will Shaw," said she in a pretty, lilting
voice that came through Mr. Mickle's lips. "Do not tease
and torment us longer with your silence, why, it is worser
far than Judy's ranting, or the baby's bawling or the dog's
yipping—that dog's a biter, too—fair warning—'ware his
teeth! Nothing yet? A *word* from you, kind Sir—we'll
have a word! A verb? An exclamatory adjective? Why,
then, a slight *cough*—that's all we ask. Well—we'll con-
tract for a nod. Give us a little nod to affirm your presence
here, or we shall conclude that you are an image dreamed
up in his loneliness by this comical fellow Mickle. Ah, I
see! That's it! You scorn him! It is for that reason you continue mum. You mislike this the fellow altogether; you
abominate his company—for that he rattles and prattles
and tootles too much!"

"No! No! I love his company!" Will said to Polly. "I
love him! He is a wonderful man!"

"Well," she said. "It's a mercy you found it out. Now,
forgive me, it is past my bedtime—"

Replacing Polly in the sack, Humphrey Mickle smiled.
"She'd get a stone talking, that one would. Now, will you
come out with me while I give LaMothe her long-overdue

supper? Then we two had best get our rest. We'll make an early start in the morning, eh?"

"I'm to go with you?" Will whispered.

"That was my offer, back there at Kip-the-Pigman's stall, if you remember. You may go with me if you like. If you wish." Better not mention the other offer. Too late now for the boy to make a choice. Mr. Mickle was confident this was the right one.

"Oh, I do, I do want to go with you," Will said. "But what will Mr. Paston say?"

"Little enough, I warrant. There be a mort of alley children he can press into service for a bed and a bit of bread."

Will shuddered. "I had no bed, Master. Straw, I had."

"A figure of speech. I am given to figures of speech, you'll find."

Will thought he'd already found that.

"You'll grow accustomed to my syntax, Will. It's affected, indeed pompous, but affords me amusement and may tickle you, too, in a lustrum or so."

"It already does," Will said shyly. "I mostly don't understand what you're saying, but I like to hear it."

"There's a start, a start. Now, for LaMothe."

In the eyeless night, in the fog, the little horse was a pale blur cropping the grass. She came softly trotting at Mr. Mickle's low whistle. He kissed her nose, patted her shoulder, put a pail of grain on the ground before her.

"That's a nice name," said Will, running his hand along her back. "LaMothe."

"My little horse, who is not, you observe, much more than a pony, is so quiet and gray that she seems to me mothlike. Think you likewise?"

"Yes. Yes, I do." For a moment poor Casper's ghost

seemed to whinny in his ear. "She's a lovely horse," said Will, and Casper disappeared.

"Therefore, I call her LaMothe. A sturdy beast, for all her smallness. She'll carry us well. Now, Will—" They returned to the caravan. When the door was closed, Mr. Mickle took a blanket from the bed. "This will be better than straw, but I trust you'll be comfortable on the floor? I am too old to bed upon it myself, except in extreme necessity—"

"It's so—so wonderful," said Will, lying down with a sigh. "I like it here on this floor very well, Master."

"One thing more, before we sink in the arms of Morpheus. I've a distaste for the word 'Master.' If you can, call me Humphrey. If not, Mr. Mickle. Agreed?"

Sighing again, Will said with a tentative smile, "Yes, Mr. Mickle. Thank you, Mr. Mickle."

"Well, there's a start," said the puppet man again. "A good start." He turned down the lamp and spoke in the darkness.

"Sleep well, Will. Sleep well."

Next to the fire, in his large, carved, commodious, cushioned chair, John Kempton, Esq., wearing a brown velvet house robe, piped with gold silk, a silken nightcap, and velvet slippers, sat with Herbert on his lap, musing over the long day just past.

He had reckoned up his accounts and found he'd done marvelous well. But for a few ells of satin, he'd sold his entire stock. He would be able to send a handsome gift to Christ Hospital for Children.

This morning—now almost yesterday morning—seemed nearly out of recall. How could he have known, when he rose to go to Bartholomew Fair, that before the day was out, he would have met the gaze of, received a nod from, great Elizabeth herself!

The Alpine moment of his life, never again to be matched! His heart thumped at the recollection. He was warmed, as with a rich cordial.

Eliza, the Queen. Gloriana. How splendid she was, walking in her array of magnificent stuffs and glittering gems, the back so erect, the eye so keen. How she sailed amidst her people, pale and beautiful as the moon traversing the sky! How she had heard him shout his love aloud in the crowd and turned her elegant head and let her eye rest upon him!

Here and there he'd heard, without minding at all, murmurs of discontent. The two Flemings, crude fellows, had earlier decried her looks, speaking aside—apparently not to offend him, their host—though perhaps that gave them too great credit. And at the moment of the Queen's observance of him, a little London urchin, a ragged, barefoot girl at his side, had cried out some comment about the Queen's teeth.

"These are people of little understanding, Herbert. Not to be heeded. Our Queen—yours, too, Sir Fur—is the quintessence of beauty, of grace, of nobility, of wit. She is the most perfect Lady that ever ruled a kingdom. . . . Kings themselves pale by compare. . . . Ah! That I should have lived to be so singled out!"

For a long time he sat, one hand on the dozing cat, staring into the fire, burning low now. Just a spurt here and there of live flame that cast shadows on the hearth.

That boy he'd given a ride to. He'd remember him, too, as part of this day. A winning lad, sturdy backed and inde-

pendent in his rags, in his hunger. Made a man want more
than ever to have a son of his own. He had even considered . . .

He reviewed the conversation that he and Humphrey
Mickle had had in Kip-the-Pigman's stall. How he'd explained that he was prepared to give the boy a home here
in his mansion and perhaps, in time, *make* it his home,
with all that that implied, but Mr. Mickle had protested
with vigor.

"Your reasons?" John Kempton inquired. "Plainly the
lad is mistreated, wherever he lodges now. If he lodges at
all. Mayhap just roams the streets, begging his bread."

"Not that," Humphrey Mickle had said.

"I'm inclined to agree. He's not a beggar. Then—inden-
tured or apprenticed or simply enslaved by someone who
overworks and underfeeds and tyrannizes over him."

"I doubt anyone could tyrannize over him," said the
puppeteer. "I've had a test of his mettle."

"You know him?" said Mr. Kempton in surprise.

"Had converse with him this morning, by chance, on
Seething Lane, where I had gone to visit my sister, she
who keeps a taproom in the vicinity. His name is Will
Shaw, and he lives with a Peter Paston, mason, who has
persuaded him that he's articled, though I am confident
there are no papers or anything like. This is just a child he
grabbed out of a ditch and put to work."

"In that case," John Kempton began, "what reason can
you advance against my giving him shelter? I'd—I'll send
him to school."

"You are an impulsive man."

"Yes. Yes, I am. And I cannot stand by and see children
suffer."

"Neither can you take every stray into your home and heart. You'd have a fair percentage of London under your roof."

"True. But this is the boy I *see* with his bones sticking through his hide. And that pinched, pasty look of hunger. It's unmistakable. It is always, is it not, the particular case and not the general misery that we are more willing to assist?"

"Do you propose to take him in as servant or son?"

"Now, Sir! Impulsive I am, but also a practical man. I should have to know him something better before I—"

Humphrey Mickle, torrentially wordy, interrupted.

"I, Squire—*I* purpose to take the boy—if he is willing, if he is willing, a factor we must allow for—I purpose, I say, to take him into my business, a respectable one, I assure you, and make him my son and heir—" He held up an arresting hand as John Kempton made to speak. "We encounter calamities, calculable and incalculable, as we mark our progress through life."

He waited for a nod of agreement, received it, and pressed on. "Should we live long enough, we grow old. I approach the time when it behooves me to eye age with respect. We all wish, do we not, to have someone to whom to pass along our art or our fortune—"

Again an attempt by John Kempton to speak, again the upraised hand. "I have no son," Humphrey Mickle said gravely.

"Nor have I."

"But you are a fairly young man yet, and of settled ways, and excellent fortune. You could create your own family. On the other hand, I am far from young or settled, but have an art to teach—puppetry *is* an art—"

"Of that I am sure."

"Anyway," Humphrey Mickle said simply, "he'd be more comfortable with me. You allow that even a ride in your carriage discommoded him."

Steadily they eyed each other across the table, across the ale and roast pork still untouched on their plates. At length John Kempton nodded, possibly with relief. "I doubt not he'd be best with you. May I—that is, I hope you do not take offense, but I am a man of means and could offer you—"

Up went the hand again. "Say no more, Sir! I appreciate your impulse, but if the boy comes with me, he is my responsibility."

"If, indeed. Have we taken into account that he may not wish to go with either of us?"

"If you'd seen or heard that journeyman of Paston's, you'd know that all the boy needs is an escape hatch. He simply hasn't an idea that any is open to him. Paston has seen to that."

Then Humphrey Mickle had got up, crossed the road, and in a moment—after some hesitation and some colloquy—led the boy back to the table.

"Eat your fill," they'd told him, ordering cider and pork and bread. The child had gobbled and gulped with no more manners than a monkey. In the end, with a word of thanks urged upon him by the puppeteer, he'd gone off in the company of Humphrey Mickle, to the world of Punch and Judy.

"Just as well, Herbert, just as well," John Kempton said now. He stroked the smooth fur gently, his voice—as there was only the cat now to hear—low and pleasant with fatigue. "Humphrey Mickle was no doubt in the right of it. I overawed the lad, and perhaps my house would have done likewise."

He looked about this room he admired to doting. "Strange, Herbert, that I was in almost as bad case when I was a boy— Well, had a home and family of meager sorts, but hungry and uncherished like that one. Will Shaw his name is. I wonder—at his age, would I have gone with me or with the puppet man? What say you?" Herbert, buzzing like a hive, butted his great head against Mr. Kempton's chin.

"Impulsive," the merchant continued. "Yes. Sometimes, Herbert, impulse should be avoided. But I think that on the whole it is best acted upon. Who knows? If I had not taken the boy in my carriage as I did, he might not have encountered the good Mr. Mickle as he and I sat at Kip-the-Pigman's table, and so had his chance to escape his wretched world. Oh, no—I forgot. Apparently they had met earlier on—on Boiling Lane, was it? In any case, they are together now, and I comfort myself to think I had no small part in the matter. Now, as for asking those two gentlemen from Flanders to be my guests at the Clothworkers' dinner, that was an impulse one might at first consider better ignored; they were not men I found congenial. But! Had I not invited them, I'd not have met the beautiful widow Vestry!"

For, next to encountering the Queen's royal gaze, the incident of most import that had happened to John Kempton this day was his introduction to the charming milliner, Eliza Vestry—what a marvel that she should be named Eliza!—by Jan Vetterer.

She had come to the dinner with her brother, a weaver of Bruges long settled in London and known to the Vetterers. Her late husband, dead a decade, had been a weaver, too. Now she kept a little shop in Ludgate, where she made and sold hats.

She was nicely favored, plump, and gracious. Lonely, he thought. Or at least alone. He'd made certain of that. She'd not seemed to find him comical or overbig or overloud, but had, in fact, fixed a gaze of admiring attention upon him. He could not recall that anyone before in his life had looked at him so. Admittedly he must have cut a figure in his new camlet suit, his flowing brown periwig, his gilt-handled sword.

"Herbert," he said, "my companion of years, by your leave, I have it in mind to go courting a widow. First, of course, discovering whether she likes cats. Who knows? I, too, like Will Shaw, may be this day embarked upon a new life. As that exceedingly loquacious Mr. Mickle said, I am not too old to begin a family of my own. To have a son, God willing!"

Putting the big cat gently on the floor, he rose, stretched, yawned. "What a day this has been, Herbert, this, the last day of Bartholomew Fair!"

He went to his bed well content, as the bells of London rang midnight.

A little later, in the street below, the watch went by, crying his message. "Past twelve o' the clock," he called, for any awake to hear, "on a thick and misty morning, and all is well. . . ."